Vote for the Class Acts couple you'd like to read about next...

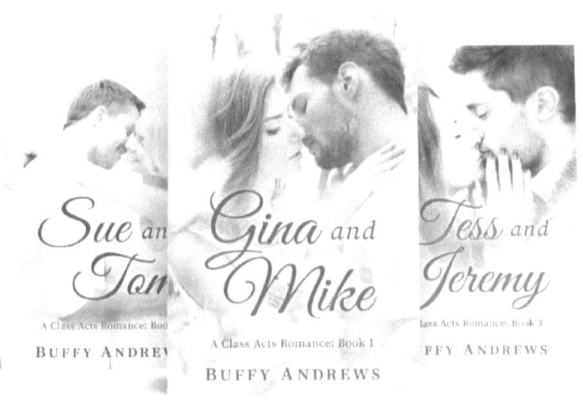

Kris and Keith

Cookie and Harry

Maggie and James

Karen and Mia

Cast your vote at http://bit.ly/35zdR9n

Also by Buffy Andrews

Sue and Tom

Class Acts

BUFFY ANDREWS

Andrews Creative Concepts
York, Pennsylvania 17404
andrewscreativeconcepts.com

Print ISBN: 978-1-7352216-4-9
Ebook ISBN: 978-1-7352216-5-6

First edition 2013, The Yearbook Series
Second edition 2020, Class Acts
Published in the United States of America

To Tania, Cindy and Dawn
the best sisters in the world!

I love you bunches and bunches! B

Chapter 1

Sue

The day I came home and found my husband in bed with our neighbor was the day I swore off men.

I heard them before I found them screwing in the bed I thought I'd sleep in forever. Turned out, I threw Steve out—and the bed along with him.

I sort of, kind of expected he was having an affair. There were little signs. Like a scratch on his back that didn't come from my nails and the faint smell of citrus-infused perfume on our silk sheets. I explained everything away. The scratch was from the dog, probably when they wrestled on the floor. And the citrus scent? That was from the fabric softener. Yeah, that's it. The fabric softener. I had an excuse for everything until the day I came home and found his ass in the air and her underneath, digging her nails into his back and coming so hard it actually made me jealous. Pathetic, I know.

It was a Friday morning, and nothing was going right. My 2-year-old daughter, Chloe, was crying hysterically for her favorite bear. I found him eventually, but not before Sneakers had chewed off the bear's ear, which only made Chloe cry more. I was late dropping Chloe off at daycare, and that made me late for work. My day went south faster than my paralegal paycheck. By the time lunch rolled around, I realized I hadn't eaten breakfast and that I'd left my sandwich on the kitchen counter. So I went home.

I was surprised to see Steve's Lexus in the driveway. He was an attorney and worked in an office across town. He had told me he'd be tied up in court all day. I figured he must be really sick because he never came home for lunch. Turned out, he was indulging in a five-star meal with a decadent dessert.

Somewhere between the bottom of the staircase and the top, I realized Steve's lunch was a midday fuck. I heard him talking dirty to Renee. I recognized her raspy voice. She lived next door with a 60-year-old who could've been her father. Steve was saying things like "bitch" and "baby" and she was screaming stuff like "fuck" and "faster."

I thought back to all of the times when Steve wanted me to talk dirty and dress like a whore. I'd tried dressing like a whore. I bought the sexiest lingerie I could find. Black with red lace. But I couldn't talk dirty. I just couldn't. I tried. Once. But I sounded so stupid it made me laugh. I even tried practicing when Steve wasn't around, but it just wasn't for me.

It wasn't long after the whore role playing that I became pregnant with Chloe, and Steve stopped wanting me. He told me I was getting fat, and that I'd better make sure after I had the baby to return to the size two he married. But it never happened. I tried, but the last ten pounds were happy hanging around and no amount of exercise or starvation seemed to chase them away. So I stayed a size eight, and Steve stayed away. And, as much as Steve loved Chloe, he seemed to loathe me more and more.

So when I found him fucking Little Miss Fake Tits with the pierced nipple (yes, I saw more than I wanted to see!) I guess I wasn't surprised.

My BFF Gina, who's an attorney, hooked me up with a killer colleague, and before Steve knew it, his mid-day fuck had cost him a shitload of money.

That was twelve years ago, and I haven't been in a serious relationship since. Sure, a few dates here and there, but nothing that I hoped would ever turn into something more.

Until now.

⌒ ⌒

"Oh my God! Oh My God! Gina." I hugged my best friend. Tears streamed down my cheeks. "I don't know what to say. I'm happy. Shocked. My God. I can't believe you're moving home. And that you're going to have a baby. Mike's baby!"

Gina sniffed. "I know. I'm shocked, too. I mean, things happened so fast between us. I didn't plan... I never thought when I left I'd be coming back so soon."

I grabbed the box of tissues off the kitchen counter, and we both took a fistful. "Guess that means no artificial insemination."

Gina laughed. "Yeah. Who would've thought?"

Gina was right. Things had happened fast between her and Mike. They were high school sweethearts, and Gina had broken up with him after our senior year, right before college started. They reconnected at our 20th high school reunion.

Turned out all of those nights spent online looking at sperm donor profiles with Gina, who planned to be a single mom, were a total waste of time. A few hot nights with the love of her life were all it took.

I was so happy for her. She was leaving her job as a prosecutor in Florida and moving back to Pennsylvania to live in the house she grew up in. Mike, and his son Jack, would move in with her. She planned to leave her job and open her own law practice here. And she wanted me to help run the office.

"Are you sure this is what you want?" I asked. "You're giving up a lot."

Gina bit her lip. "No, I'm gaining a lot. You. Chloe. Mike. The people I love most in the world are here. If there's one thing I've learned, it's that life is for living. I've never felt about anyone the way I feel about Mike. Even after all these years he still makes my body quiver just thinking about him. And now I'm going to have his baby."

Gina placed the palm of her hand over her stomach, and the tears flooded her eyes again. "Mike's baby," Gina said. "I'm going to have Mike's baby."

"And I'm almost certain that getting pregnant the old-fashioned way definitely felt better than having a catheter stuck up you vagina—and cheaper, too."

Gina laughed. "I love you, Sues."

"I love you, too."

Gina took a sip of tea. "So how's Tom?"

I smiled. I'd been doing that a lot lately. "He's pretty incredible. I'm not used to being treated so well. He's kind, thoughtful. We've been on a dozen dates and he hasn't tried to get me in bed."

Gina's eyes widened. "Really?"

I nodded. "And I've been so damn horny it's driving me crazy. I'm beginning to think something's wrong with me. Maybe I'm not sexy enough. God knows I was never sexy enough for Steve, even when I dressed like the whore he wanted me to be."

"Oh, God, Sues," Gina said. "Nothing's wrong with you. You're a woman. You have needs. Maybe he's waiting for you to make the first move. He always was a little shy."

"Do you think so?"

"Yeah, I do. I mean, he's liked you forever. He finally gets a shot, and he doesn't want to blow it."

"So what should I do?"

Gina pointed her finger at me. "You take the lead. Seduce him."

"I'm not sure I remember how. It's been forever since I came on to a guy. After being rejected by Steve, I never wanted to take the chance."

Gina waved her hand. "Oh God, girl. Just watch some pay-per-view. That'll get you in the mood, and once you're in the mood, just relax and let go. Besides, I have a feeling that once you come on to him it won't take long before you're rolling between the sheets. I bet you a hundred bucks he's waiting for you to make the first move. So make it. Shave and get ready for some wild sex."

I bit my lip. "It is tempting. He's coming over later, and Chloe's going to her dad's."

"Which means you'll have the entire house to yourself. And you can be as loud as you want."

We both laughed. It was so good to have Gina standing in my kitchen. I'd forgotten how easy it is to talk to her about my sex life—or lack thereof. We were soul sisters, and I was so glad she was moving home and would be closer. And I knew Chloe would be, too.

The back door opened. "Hi, Mom," Chloe said.

"Look who's here!"

"Aunt Gina." Chloe ran over to hug her godmother.

Gina wrapped her arms around Chloe. "Hi, sweetie."

"What are you doing here?"

"It's a long story," Gina said. "We'll talk later."

"Is everything okay?" Chloe asked.

"Everything's perfect," Gina said. "Just perfect."

Chloe turned to me. "Did Dad call?"

I nodded. "He said to tell you he'd pick you up after work. And he's taking you to that Italian restaurant you love."

"Great," Chloe said. "I'm starved."

Chloe went to change clothes, and I walked Gina to her car. "So when do you think you'll be able to move?"

"A month. Maybe two. Not soon enough, that's for sure."

I hugged Gina. "I love you."

"I love you, too," Gina said. "And just be yourself with Tom. He cares about you a lot. And I have a feeling you're falling for him. So maybe, just maybe, this might be your second chance. And if it is, I don't want you blowing it."

"Sounds like something I told you not too long ago.'

Gina smiled. "It was. And it was good advice."

I watched Gina pull away, and I couldn't stop grinning. My best friend was coming home. And the guy I was falling for was coming over. And I was going to have sex!

Chapter 2

Tom

"I'm sorry, boy." I scratched Klondike's head. My 12-year-old lab wanted to play some more, but I had to shower. I told Sue I'd be over by 7. I felt bad that I wasn't spending as much time with him. But man, was I happy where I *was* spending my time.

I'd always liked Sue, ever since junior high when we were lab partners in earth science and had to dissect a worm. For the record, I did most of the dissecting. Sue mostly held her nose and fake barfed so I had to do all the incisions and pin the flaps to the black wax in the aluminum dissecting tray.

Anyway, in high school I wanted to ask Sue out, but she always had a boyfriend. Truth is, I'm kind of shy. I didn't date much back then. In fact, I'm sure I was one of the few virgins in my freshmen dorm in college. I had a few relationships that had potential, one especially. Even got engaged. Thank God I called it off before I said "I do." Rachel was more high maintenance than my '58 MG I'd completely restored. So, I called it quits a little over a year ago. Boy, was she pissed. When I went over to her apartment to pick up my things, I found them littered on the lawn. She had thrown everything out of her third-floor window.

Sue is so different from anyone I've ever been with. Especially Rachel. Rachel always made me feel like I never measured up, that things were never good enough. Like when we went on vacation. I'd choose a moderately priced hotel, not because I was cheap but because I didn't see the need to shell out the extra money for amenities I could do without. But Rachel wanted the most expensive, not because she necessarily cared about the fluffy bathrobe the hotel provided, but for the bragging rights.

I remember one blow-up in particular where she refused to go inside the hotel when we arrived because she said it was only a four-star and not a five. I was so embarrassed that I finally went inside, canceled our reservation, and went to the five-star down the beach. She was a spoiled bitch, the only child of a doctor I served with on the YMCA board.

The Great Hotel Standoff, as it became known, was the beginning of the end. That's when I really started to question if Rachel was worth it. Turned out, she wasn't. For me, the standoff was a wake-up call, like having a bucket of ice water thrown on you unexpectedly on a hot day. After the surprise makes you jump, you realize that it feels damn good.

Despite living in the same town, I hadn't run into Sue much over the years. She wasn't one of the regulars at the pharmacy where I worked. But when I saw her at our class reunion, all my old feelings came rushing back. Maybe I would've felt differently if she had changed, but she was the same fun-loving Sue. Gorgeous smile. Long blonde hair that looks great even when it's messy. And a petite body that's more gymnast than ballerina but still as sexy as hell.

We'd been on about a dozen dates so far, but I haven't made the big move yet. It's not that I don't want to be with her. I do. More than anything. But I want to make sure I don't pressure her. I want her to want it as much as I do. I sense that she does, but I want to be absolutely sure. This is one relationship I definitely don't want to mess up. I'm looking for more than sex here—and I'm sort of hoping Sue is, too.

I gurgled and spit out the minty mouthwash as Klondike watched from his spot near the sunken tub. I leaned in close to the mirror to examine my face. No nose hairs sticking out; good. I rubbed my palm over my face. "Think I should shave, boy?"

Klondike cocked his big, soft head and whimpered. I know he didn't like coming in second. I reached down and scratched his head. "I know I have it bad, boy. But this girl's special. Not like any of the others."

Klondike seemed to like Sue. He didn't growl at her like he'd constantly growled at Rachel. In fact, when Sue and Chloe came to dinner last week, Klondike cozied up to her. The only time he left Sue's side was when Chloe took him for a walk.

I played tug with Klondike a little more before leaving him lying on the sofa.

On my way over to Sue's, I stopped to buy a bottle of her favorite wine. Figured that might help to set the mood. I knew Chloe was spending the night at her dad's, and I was sort of hoping that tonight might be the night.

∽∽

Sue

"Dad's here," Chloe yelled from the front door.
I ran into the living room to kiss Chloe goodbye.
Steve nodded. "Hi, Sue."

I hated how his dark eyes scanned my body from head to toe. "You look well."

I smiled. "Thanks. I feel great."

Chloe grabbed her backpack off the couch. "Mom's dating someone."

I rolled my eyes. I could always count on Chloe to spill the beans to her dad. "Chloe, it's no big deal. It's just an old friend."

"Someone she went to high school with," Chloe said.

Steve eyebrows jumped. "Anyone I know?"

I shook my head. "We reconnected at my high school reunion. We're just friends."

"And Aunt Gina's moving home," Chloe blurted out again.

"Really?" Steve asked. He looked at me. "Gina's leaving Florida?"

I nodded. "Yeah, she's coming home and starting over."

"Wow. I didn't see that coming," Steve said.

"I don't think any of us did. But we're super glad about it."

"Well, good for her," Steve said. "And good for you and Chloe. I know how much you both love her."

Steve looked at Chloe. "Ready to go, Princess?"

I hugged Chloe and kissed her cheek. "Bye, sweetie. See you tomorrow after school."

As I watched Steve and Chloe walk to his car, I was reminded of how much they look alike. Chloe had Steve's chocolate eyes and his chestnut hair. And she was already a good six inches taller than me. I was a hair over five feet. Even got back to a size 2 after the divorce and managed to stay that size just to spite Steve. But I always envied the girls with willowy limbs.

I grabbed my shaver off the vanity and jumped in the shower. Tom would be here in a half hour, and I had to get my sexiness on.

"Damn razor!" I pulled off another square of toilet paper and stuck it on my bleeding leg, right below my knee. Of all days to cut myself. Ugh!

My knees were battle worn as it was. I was a gymnast and cheerleader in high school and by the time my senior year had ended, I'd torn the medial meniscus in both knees. Besides those scars, I had ones from a bad spill I took while running on asphalt as a kid. I chewed up my knee so badly that the doctor used small metal clips that looked like staples to close the gaping holes. I still had a few pieces of asphalt embedded in my knee. So, yeah, my knees aren't pretty.

"Shit." Just when I got the blood stopped in my knee, I found a white hair growing out of my chin. This called for some reinforcements. I grabbed my cell phone and called Gina.

"You what?" Gina asked. "I can barely hear you. We took Jack out for pizza, and it's noisy in here."

I shouted into my cell phone. "I said, there's a white hair coming out of my chin! A freakin' wiry white hair about an inch long."

I could hear Gina laugh.

"It's not funny. Oh God. First I cut my leg shaving, and now I find a white hair sticking out of my chin."

"Just pull it," Sue said.

"I did. That's not the point. The point is, how long do you think it's been there? What if Tom saw the white hair and just didn't say anything? God, I'm so embarrassed. I feel like that old woman in *Snow White*."

"She had a wart on her nose, not a hair on her chin," Gina said.

"Same difference. It wasn't supposed to be there. Wart. Stray facial hair. It's all the same. What if there are other things on me that aren't supposed to be there? Like a hairy mole on my ass."

Gina laughed. "So you're planning on showing him your ass?"

"At this point, I'm afraid to show him any part of my naked self."

I could hear Gina tell Mike she was going to the bathroom. I chewed my lip, waiting for her to return.

"Are you there?" asked Gina a few minutes later.

"Of course I'm here. I need help. A white hair growing out of my chin is no small matter."

"Listen," Gina said. "Don't panic. You're nervous about tonight. You plucked it, so it's gone. I didn't see a white hair coming out of your chin when I saw you earlier. And believe me, I would've noticed it."

"Are you sure?"

"Positive. Don't I notice everything?"

"True. You do. But do they grow that fast?"

Gina cleared her throat. "Yes, they're like weeds. They spring up when you're not looking. So quit freakin' out. It could be worse. Remember Cookie's inverted nipple?"

I'd forgotten about Cookie's inverted nipple and how she used sex toys and suction cups and clamps to try to coax it out. She eventually had to have surgery.

"Okay. Point taken. White hair and shaver cut don't come close to Cookie's inverted nipple. Thanks for putting things in perspective. Now, go back and enjoy your pizza. And don't you dare tell Mike why I called."

Gina laughed. "I won't. And I'll call tomorrow to find out how the sex was. In the meantime, relax and enjoy it. You deserve to have one hell of an orgasm."

Chapter 3

Tom

When Sue opened the door, she looked so damn sexy. Her hair was in a messy ponytail, high on her head. I loved the carefree look. She wore old blue jeans that had a hole in the thigh and were frayed at the bottom. I could see she wasn't wearing a bra under her white cotton blouse. And she was barefoot. Even her pink polished toes looked sexy. God, I had it bad for this girl. I wanted to throw her down on the floor right then.

The ends of Sue's mouth curled up, and her lips seemed plumper. "Hi, Tom. I'm so glad to see you."

"Really?" I asked. "Is something wrong?"

Sue shook her head. "Nothing now that you're here."

I handed Sue the wine and followed her into the kitchen. She fetched two wine glasses from the cupboard and filled the glasses.

"Remember that time in high school a bunch of us got Gina's neighbor to buy us Boone's Farm Wild Cherry wine and we went to the lake?"

I laughed. "That stuff was nasty."

"Yeah, but it was the only thing we could afford. And it got us wasted. Fast."

"And sick the next day," I said.

"True. I remember throwing up all over my white shirt. The stains never did come out. I wonder if they still make that stuff."

I took a sip of the zinfandel I'd brought. "I have no intention of finding out."

"Are you hungry?" Sue asked.

I shook my head. "I ate with Klondike."

"How's he doing, anyway?"

"Great, except I think he's sad I'm not spending as much time as I used to with him."

"Well, bring him along with you when you come over," Sue said.

"Really?"

"Sure. I don't mind. I grew up with dogs. In fact, I bought one right after Steve and I were married. Steve wasn't happy about it. He's more of a cat person. But I loved Sneakers. He passed away when Chloe was 10, and we were both devastated. Guess that's why we never got another one. Too painful. "

"So that's why Chloe was so anxious to take Klondike on a walk."

"Yes, she loves dogs, but when Sneakers died, she had a really tough time."

"Rachel hated Klondike," I blurted out before I realized how uncool it was to bring up my ex.

"She sounds like a real piece of work," said Sue, licking off the sweet wine that pickled her lips.

I rolled my eyes. "She was. And I realize that now more than ever. She was the most self-centered person I'd ever dated. And it took me a long time to see that. What about you? You have any horror stories—I mean, besides your marriage."

⌒〜

Sue

I wasn't sure how much to tell Tom. I wanted to tell him everything. About finding Steve in bed with Miss Fake Tits with the pierced nipple. About Steve fighting me for custody of Chloe. About the affairs I'd learned about after we divorced—Miss Fake Tits was one of many. But I didn't want to ruin the mood or spend the night talking about the past. I wanted to concentrate on the present, do what Gina told me to do. Relax and let go.

I put some cheese and crackers on a plate, and Tom grabbed the wine. We went to my sunroom to sit and chat.

"So do you get embarrassed at your job?"

"Where did that come from?"

I shrugged my shoulders. "Oh, I don't know. I was just thinking about the time I had to buy vaginal cream at the pharmacy and there was a male cashier. I was sort of embarrassed."

Tom smiled. "Believe me, we pharmacists don't gossip about what customers buy. We really don't care. So many people don't ask questions because they're too embarrassed. But I'd rather have them ask. Like the other day. A woman asked which condoms were best."

"A condom conundrum, eh?"

Tom laughed. "That's one way to put it."

I smiled. I couldn't picture Tom explaining the pros and cons of particular condoms. But in the last few weeks, I'd seen a side of him I hadn't before. Yes, he was the shy guy with brains from high school. But he had definitely loosened up and was more fun than I remembered him being back in the day. "So what did you tell her?"

Tom shrugged. "I told her it depends but recommended ones made out of Microsheer. They're thinner. And they come with the normal bells and whistles if you want that."

"Normal bells and whistles?" I was enjoying watching Tom's face turn the color of my toenails.

"Yeah. You know. Ribbed ones. Colored ones. Even flavored ones."

I scrunched my nose. "Sorry, but licking a cherry-flavored condom would be like licking a cherry Blow Pop. I'd rather have what's inside without having to work so dang hard to get it."

Tom laughed. "You're crazy, you know that."

"Oh, that reminds me of a story Gina told me, but she would kill me if I shared it."

"Oh, no," Tom said. "You're not gonna do that."

"What?" I teased.

"Leave me hanging about what Gina told you. That's not playing fair."

"Okay, but you have to promise not to tell her I told you."

Tom nodded.

"So she was with this guy one time and things were getting really hot and heavy and he pulls out this condom. Turned out it was a glow-in-the-dark condom. He thought it would be a fun surprise, but Gina couldn't help but laugh and the moment was lost. When she finally got it back, she said she felt like she was screwing a kid's glow stick."

Tom laughed. "Either that or a light saber."

I totally lost it. I couldn't stop laughing. It was a good thing I didn't have a swig of wine in my mouth because I would've spit it out all over Tom. "Actually, a glow stick is probably more accurate. Gina said he had a pencil dick."

Tom laughed. "For the record, I don't do glow in the dark."

Tom

I watched Sue laugh so hard she had tears coming out of her eyes. I don't think I've ever been with anyone who's more fun. She just says what's on her mind, and I love that about her. I think I've laughed more since we've started dating than I have my whole life. It probably wasn't the right time to bring up her ex-husband, but I wondered what had happened.

I couldn't imagine Sue not getting along with anyone. But I also knew she was fiercely aggressive when it came to protecting those she cared about. I remember in high school Mike had told me about an incident at a party. Gina wasn't at the party and he got drunk, was horny, and ended up naked with a girl who had come on to him. Sue barged into the bedroom and stopped the action. Mike was glad for the save, and said Sue never let him forget what an asshole he'd been.

"Can I ask you something?" I asked.

Sue dabbed her tears and straightened up. "Sure. Is it going to make me laugh again?"

I shook my head. "What happened in your marriage?"

"Do you want the short version or the long version?"

"Whichever version you want to give me."

Sue took a deep breath. "Then we'll go with the medium. I loved Steve. I thought I'd be married to him forever. But when I became pregnant with Chloe, he stopped wanting me. At first, I thought it had something to do with the baby. Like maybe he was afraid of hurting her or something. But after Chloe was born, it was more of the same. He said I was too fat, that I needed to lose weight. Never mind that he was the one who made me that way."

I shook my head. "I'm sorry you had to deal with that. That's awful."

"Yeah, well, it got worse. One day I came home to get the lunch I'd left on the kitchen counter. Turned out Steve was having lunch, too. Only he was having lunch in bed with the trophy wife of our 60-year-old neighbor. So, I threw him out and swore off men."

"Until now?" I asked.

Sue smirked. "Yeah. Until now. That was twelve years ago and the cut took a long time to heal. Normally, I'm a confident person. But Steve always made me feel like I never measured up, like I was never good enough. And I found myself always trying to please him."

"Like me with Rachel."

"Exactly. Like you with Rachel. Why is it that people like you and me end up with losers like them?"

"I wish I knew," I said. "Bad luck, I guess."

Sue continued. "After the divorce, I decided I'd focus on my career and Chloe. So, that's what I've done. I've had a few dates, but nothing serious. It's hard for me to open up and trust people. I trusted Steve, and look where it got me." Sue shook her head. "Well, at least I got Chloe. She's the best of both of us."

"You've done a great job raising her," I said.

"Thanks. She's my world."

"Did you ever think about having more children?" I asked.

"Sure. But when my marriage went to hell that pretty much was the end of that."

"What about you?"

"Yeah, I wanted kids. But. Well. The chances were never good I'd be able to father any. I have something to tell you. It's not easy for me to talk about it."

Sue sat up even straighter. "Tom, is everything okay?"

"It is now."

Sue sat down her glass of wine, and I sat down mine. I turned toward her. I'd planned to tell her before our relationship proceeded to sex, sort of figured I'd have to because she'd see that something was obviously missing.

Now it was my turn to take a big breath. "About ten years ago, I had testicular cancer."

Sue's hand flew to her heart. "I'm so sorry. I had no idea."

I held up my hand. "It's okay. I'm okay. It's not something I went around telling people. And being shy and quiet worked to my advantage. But I had to have one of my testicles removed and underwent chemo. At the time, I was given the opportunity to preserve some of my sperm. But I didn't think there was a point. I had no one special in my life, and the last thing on my mind was having a kid. But, yeah, I would've loved to have had a son or daughter."

I could see Sue's eyes turning glassy. She pursed her lips. "You would've made a great dad. You could always adopt. Do you know Gina was adopted?"

"I'd forgotten that," Tom said. "And I did adopt. I adopted Klondike from the animal shelter. He's my child."

Sue smiled and inched toward me. I was relieved I'd told her about the cancer. I'd been dreading it. It was so awkward to talk about something so personal, something that made me feel as if I wasn't completely whole. But when I felt Sue's lips touch mine, I knew it would be all right and that the night was just beginning.

Chapter 4

Sue

I could tell by the crackle in Tom's voice and his slight hesitation that sharing his battle with cancer was difficult. And I wondered who knew because anytime anything happened to someone in our class, news about it spread faster than a computer virus.

I was beginning to realize I was going to have to make the first move if our relationship was going to progress beyond kissing. I knew Tom wanted it as much as I did, but I also knew he'd wait for me to make the first move. He wouldn't want to take the chance he'd scare me away. So, I took Gina's advice and relaxed. The wine helped, too, and the fact that he looked so damn sexy. By the size of his biceps, he must lift weights a lot. They bulged beneath his T-shirt.

As I inched closer, my body tingled. It'd been a long time since I'd been with anyone and, to be honest, I was nervous. I didn't want to disappoint Tom. What if I didn't turn him on? What if I didn't measure up to others he'd been with? I never thought about these things before my marriage to Steve imploded. But when that happened, I couldn't help but blame myself. I figured if I'd been sexier, better in bed, that maybe Steve wouldn't have looked elsewhere. I know it sounds stupid, but that's what I thought. Steve really did a number on my self-esteem.

I stared into Tom's eyes as I inched closer, and as I leaned forward to touch his lips, I felt his arms wrap around me. The kisses went from playful to probing, our tongues danced fast and furious. It was as if all of the longing we had for each other burst in seconds. I felt him nibble my ear and his lips trail down my neck. God, he made me feel so damn sexy, and I wanted him.

"Want to pick this up someplace more comfortable?" I asked. "Wouldn't want to put on a show for the neighbors."

Just then Tom scooped me up. Being petite does have its advantages. "Tell me where you want to go," he whispered.

"Up the stairs and to the left."

I kissed Tom's neck as he carried me to my bedroom. When he laid me down on my bed, I pulled him toward me, kissing him long and hard. I reached down and felt his hardness. I started to unzip his jeans.

"I'll get it," he said.

As he took off his jeans, I pulled off my blouse and tossed it aside. Our chests touched, and Tom's mouth found my nipple. I moaned. God, it had been so long. I reached under his boxers and ran my hand over his hardness. He eased off my underwear and then his own. I felt his hardness against my leg.

"God, I want you," he whispered.

He was kissing me and touching me in places I never knew could bring me such pleasure.

"Please," I whispered. "Quit teasing me. I..."

Tom penetrated, and it was like nothing I'd ever felt before. I'd never had a lover like him, and I'd never lost control the way I was losing it now. But I couldn't help myself. I could feel his passion, and it matched my own. I tried to hold on, but I couldn't, and we climaxed together. *Wow!* I thought. So *this* is what it's really supposed to be like.

The rest of the night was a blur of kissing and sex more times than I'd ever had in one night. Tom was an amazing lover, and I was sad in a way that it took me so many years to realize what I'd been missing.

Tom

I loved feeling Sue quiver and let go. I'm not going to lie. I'd thought about making love to her a lot over these past couple of weeks. But I didn't want to push her. And when she told me about Steve cheating on her, I really wanted everything to be perfect the first time we made love. I know it was for me, and by the way she moaned and grabbed my back, I'm pretty sure it was for her, too.

God, she made me feel young again. I haven't performed like that since I was a teen! Well, technically I was a sophomore in college when I lost my virginity. The girl was a senior and very experienced. It was a hook-up. We were as drunk as could be and found ourselves alone when everyone else took off to make out. I was clumsy and came too fast. I could tell the girl was very disappointed. So, after that, I sort of took it upon myself to get schooled. Not that I had sex with girls, but I read a lot about what girls liked and didn't like. That sort of thing.

I woke up before Sue and watched her sleep. She was so beautiful, and I wanted her in my arms again. She looked like a doll next to my six-four frame. Her blonde hair fanned out across her shoulder. She began to stir and, as if suddenly remembering where she was and with whom, her eyelids popped open.

"For a minute there, I thought last night was a dream," she said sleepily.

I brushed her hair off her face. "I hope it wasn't because it was an incredible night."

A sexy smile slid onto her face. "Want to make it an incredible morning?"

I took her in my arms once again, and it was almost noon when we jumped in the shower—together.

Sue

I watched Tom pull away from the house. He had called a neighbor to take Klondike out and had planned to spend the rest of the day with him. We were going to meet Gina and Mike for a late dinner. Tomorrow was Sunday, and Gina was heading back to Florida to work on the move. Chloe called and told me her dad had bought her a couple of new outfits at this expensive store in the mall that I refuse to take her to. It's way more than I can afford.

As much as I loathed Steve, he'd always treated Chloe like a princess. Sometimes I worried that he spoiled her too much, but she never seemed to act as if she was entitled. And she understood I couldn't give her the things her dad could.

Lately, I noticed she was spending hours in the bathroom. I think that had to do with Rob moving in down the street. His family moved from Texas to Pennsylvania when his dad was transferred. Rob seemed nice enough, but Chloe was only 14. He was a couple of years older, and I wasn't happy about the age difference. So far, they'd just spent time talking, mostly at our house out of my hearing range. But I had a feeling Rob was going to ask her out one of these days, and that scared me. Steve didn't want Chloe to date until she was 16. Having dated when I was Chloe's age, I thought that was a little strict. I knew it was only a matter of time before Steve and I had to come to some kind of resolution, and we'd never been good at that—especially where Chloe is concerned.

I heard the back door open and Gina yell.

"I'm in the kitchen!" I yelled back. I filled the tea kettle and turned it on.

Gina walked in carrying a big smile. "So, tell me about Tom and don't leave anything out. I want every detail, even the details you think I don't want to know I want to know."

I arched my eyebrows. "Everything?"

"Absolutely."

I rolled my eyes. "He's the most caring man I've ever been with—unlike Steve, who only cared about his own needs."

"Makes a difference, doesn't it?" Gina asked.

"Big difference. With Steve, I was always worried about doing everything right, pleasing him in all of the ways he wanted me to. It was all about him and never about me and what I wanted. But with Tom, it's different." I smiled, remembering last night.

"I know that look," Gina said. "Come on. Tell me."

"I'm half afraid to. I don't want to jinx it. I want to feel that way again."

"Are you serious?" Gina asked. "It was *that* good?"

"It's was better than good. It was amazing. If I could live on orgasms like I had last night, I'd spend my entire life having sex!"

We laughed.

"I've never felt that way before. I didn't know I could feel that way. My body just trembled. It was like I was having my own personal earthquake. God, I had no idea what I'd been missing all of these years. Steve really was a lousy lay!"

Gina smiled. "I'm so happy for you. And for Tom, too. I still can't believe the two of you got together. And now that you are, it seems as if you were always meant to be. Does that make sense?"

I nodded. "Completely."

"Are we still on for dinner later?"

"Yep."

"So another hot night?" Gina asked.

I smiled. "I swear I feel like I'm 17 again. I'm actually a little sore."

Gina laughed. "But at least it's a good sore, if there is such a thing."

The tea kettle whistled, and I filled Gina's mug. "So what did you, Mike, and Jack do last night?"

"After the pizza, we watched a movie."

"Which one?"

"An oldie but goodie. *Jaws.*"

I sipped my coffee. "God, I haven't seen that in years."

"Me, neither," Gina said. "Turned out Mike had it and Jack had never seen it, so we watched it together. I actually fell asleep. I've been so tired lately."

"I remember being tired with Chloe. It got better in the second trimester, but I was whipped for the first three months. Did you tell Jack about the baby?"

Gina laughed. "Yes. He made us promise not to put the baby in the room next to him. Said he had to put up with his sister crying at his Mom's."

I laughed. "Gotta love that kid."

"Yeah. He's pretty neat. He also put in a request for a boy. He wants a brother. Said girls are too fussy and cry all the time. He figured boys aren't like that."

I laughed. "Did you tell him that's already been decided?"

Gina shook her head. "I figured that's a conversation for Mike to have."

"What do you want?" I asked.

Gina waved her hand. "When I was going to have a child on my own through insemination, I wanted a girl. I thought it would be easier. But now that I became pregnant the old-fashioned way and the dad is in the picture, the baby's sex doesn't matter to me. Just as long as it's healthy."

"So are you going to find out the sex?"

Gina sipped her tea. "I haven't decided yet. I kind of want to know but Mike doesn't. He said it doesn't matter if it's a girl or a boy and finding out at the end gives us something to look forward to. I, on the other hand, am a planner. I'd like to know what I'm having so I can plan the nursery accordingly. So, I guess we'll have to come to some sort of compromise."

I laughed. "Something tells me you'll find out."

"What? Don't think I'm a great compromiser?"

"Well, you usually win your cases."

Chapter 5

Tom

I'd made reservations at a ritzy place that overlooked the river. I'm more of a meat and potatoes guy, but I wanted to splurge on Sue. Plus, I figured we could celebrate Gina moving back home.

When I picked up Sue, she was wearing a black dress with spaghetti straps that made my jaw drop. Her hair was in a loose bun on top of her head and strands fell to her shoulders. She looked incredibly sexy.

"You look great," I said. "I love your dress."

She waved her hand. "Oh, this ratty old thing. It's been in my closet forever. I don't get many opportunities to wear it."

"Well, you look amazing."

"So how was your day with Klondike?" she asked, offering me a glass of wine.

"I think I'm back on his good side—for now. I took him to the park, and he ran into some old friends. We threw some Frisbee and I bought him some ice cream doggie treats at the store. When I left, he was sleeping on the couch."

Sue sipped her wine. "Sounds like the two of you had a nice day."

"What'd you do?" I asked.

"Gina stopped over, and we gabbed for a while."

I rolled my eyes. "I'm sure you told her everything."

Sue smiled. "Well, she *is* my best friend."

I shifted in my seat. "Mike was right about you two."

Sue scrunched her eyes. "What's that supposed to mean?"

"He said you guys tell each other everything."

"I suppose that's true," Sue said. "Except for that bastard raping her. That she didn't tell me."

"She didn't tell anyone," I said.

"But you knew, and you didn't say anything."

I held up my hand. "Oh, no. You're not going to get me into that conversation again."

When Sue learned I knew about our math teacher raping Gina in high school, she wasn't happy I hadn't told anyone. Looking back, I wish I had. But at the time, my 17-year-old self felt that it was Gina's story to tell, not mine. Anyway, Sue and I had a long talk about it, and I didn't want to have another long talk about it. It was in the past and there was nothing we could do to change it.

"Sorry. You're right. We don't need to go there again. Especially when we can go here."

Sue leaned in and kissed me. I just about spilled my wine on her damn sexy black dress.

Sue

I could tell by the way Tom scanned my body that he liked the black dress I'd bought that afternoon. I didn't want him to know that I had run to the upscale clothing store in the mall to get something to wear after Gina left. When he told me where he was taking me, I checked my closet for something sexy and found nothing but frumpy grandma clothes. I wanted to wear something that made a statement. Something that said "I've got something that you want—bad!"

I think every girl should have a little black dress—and not the kind you wear to funerals. I also bought a push-up bra that made my boobs look bigger. I have to admit, I was feeling pretty good about myself.

Gina and Mike were waiting for us at the bar when we arrived at the inn. Gina looked her normal knock-out self in a white strapless dress. I love her in white. It shows off her beautiful red hair and emerald eyes.

Mike jumped off the bar stool and offered it to me. I hugged Gina.

"Love the dress," she whispered in my ear. "It's perfect."

The bartender walked over. "What can I get you?"

I looked at Gina. "What are you having?"

"Sticking with diet tonic. Nine months of not drinking is going to be a bitch."

I smiled. "Yeah, but when you hold that baby in your arms, it'll be worth it."

I decided to have another glass of Chardonnay.

It wasn't long before the waiter showed us to our table. We were next to a huge window with a gorgeous view of the river. I had heard people talk about this place, but I'd never been here. It's one of those places most people I know only go to for something really special—like a wedding anniversary. The average entrée was forty bucks. I sort of felt bad that Tom was spending so much money on the meal, but I knew he wanted to.

Gina ordered a bottle of champagne. When the waiter went to fill her glass, she placed her hand over it. "Fill mine with water."

Gina lifted her glass. "To great friends. I hope life brings you everything you've ever wanted."

We all cheered and touched our glasses. When Tom took a sip of champagne, his eyes grew wider and he choked, spitting it out all over the table.

"I'm so sorry." Tom stood up, dabbing the tablecloth with his linen napkin.

"What's the matter, Tom?" a woman said. "Surprised to see me?"

The woman was probably the sexiest woman in the entire place. Her silky black dress with a slit up the leg and X-rated neckline (I swear her boobs looked like they were going to fall out!) clung to her hour-glass figure like plastic wrap. She made me look like Cinderella in black rags—and my push-up bra enhanced boobs were baseballs compared to her basketballs!

Tom coughed. "Rachel. Hi."

Rachel ran her long tongue over her ruby lips. "Aren't you going to introduce me to your friends?" She scanned the table, working her sexy smile. I realized who she was and wanted to smack that smile right off her picture-perfect, not-a-thing-out-of-place Barbie face.

"Uh, sure," Tom stuttered. "This is Sue, Gina, and Mike. Friends of mine from high school. And this is Rachel, an old friend."

She put her hands on her hips. "Excuse me, darling. I'm more than an old friend, wouldn't you say? I mean, after all, we were engaged!" And then the bitch winked.

Rachel must've seen my eyes jump to the top of my forehead because she quickly excused herself. "Well, my date is waiting. He's a surgeon, and I want to make sure I'm the only one he's operating on tonight."

She glided away, putting one foot in front of the other and striding from the hips. Yep! She had the seductive walk nailed. I definitely had to work on that. When I walk, I suck in my stomach trying to make it look flatter, but then my damn ass sticks out way too far.

Tom shook his head. "I'm sorry about that. But now you've met Rachel."

I put my napkin on the table. "I'll be right back. I need to use the ladies' room."

Tom

I looked at Mike and ran my fingers through my hair. "Guess I fucked up."

"You hadn't told Sue that you were engaged to that piece of work?"

"I meant to, just never got around to it. And you know how Rachel is."

"Yeah, I know how Rachel is. That's why I can't believe you didn't tell Sue about her."

"I told her some, just not the engaged part."

"Did you tell her about the cancer?" Mike asked.

I nodded. "Sort of had to, if you know what I mean. But I just didn't feel like going into the whole near-wedding saga."

"You mean that you practically left Rachel standing at the altar when you called off the wedding a month before?" Mike said.

"Okay. I get your point. I was going to tell Sue. Just not yet. Does Gina know about Rachel?"

Mike shook his head. "Of course not. I had no reason to fill her in on the assorted details of that fucked up affair. And personally, you made the right call, even if you did wait until the last minute."

"So what do I do now?"

"When they come back, tell Sue you're sorry and that you'll talk later. That it's been over between you and Rachel for a long time, and you want to focus on enjoying the evening with her and your friends."

Sue

I was mad, and Gina knew it. I marched into the ladies' room, and she followed.

"Wait." She held up her hand. Gina checked the stalls to make sure we were alone.

"She was a real piece of work," Gina said. "She worked her skinny-ass body like a whore on the strip."

I bared my teeth. "Did you see the way she looked at Tom? I wanted to smack that smile right off her face. Oh, and the fact that they were engaged. Seriously? I had no idea Tom had ever been engaged."

"You mean he never told you about Rachel?"

"He told me a little about Rachel. Said she was self-centered and spoiled. But he never told me he was going to marry her."

"Thank God he didn't," Gina said. "That never would've lasted. One look at her and I can see that girl is high maintenance."

"I agree. She's not his type. But am I?"

Gina put her arms on my shoulders and looked me straight in the eyes. "You are an amazing person. I know that Tom really cares about you. Don't let his ex-girlfriend..."

"Fiancé," I clarified.

"Don't let his ex-fiancé come between you. Stake your claim, and if she gets too close, it's smackdown time."

"But did you see her? She's gorgeous."

"You're gorgeous," Gina said. "You look amazing tonight. Now, we're going back to the table. Own it, sister. And if that bitch shows up at our table again, have a comeback ready."

"Like what?"

"Oh, I don't know," Gina said. "Maybe you compliment her dress and tell her you saw one just like it at the thrift store. That ought to deflate her tits a little."

"Do you think her girls are real?"

"Not a chance," Gina said. "They're as fake as her nails."

I looked at my nails. "At least she has nails. I have stubs."

"And you have gorgeous stubs."

Tom

When the girls returned to the table, Mike and I stood to pull out their chairs.

"Such gentlemen," Gina smiled.

Sue's face still looked a little red but at least she smiled.

"So, what's everyone having?" Mike asked, trying to lighten the mood. "The waiter said the Peruvian red tail bass has been selling well."

Sue held up her hand. "I can't do fish. My grandfather traumatized me when I was a kid. I sat beside him at a restaurant once and when the waiter served his fish, it still looked like a fish."

Mike laughed. "What was it supposed to look like? A fish stick?"

"Yes, that I would've eaten. This fish still had its eyeball in it, and my grandfather teased me that he was going to eat it. I haven't eaten fish since."

"You don't know what you're missing," I said. "I love fish, although I've never eaten fish eyeballs. Saw someone do it once, though. Sucked them right out of the eye sockets."

Sue held up her hand. "No more or I'll puke. Just thinking about that nauseates me."

"I'm with Sue. Let's talk about something else. Something fun," Gina said.

Sue jumped up and down in her seat. "I know. I know. What is something you've never done but would like to try?"

Mike smirked. "Can it be anything?"

Sue nodded.

"Well, I read something about helicopter sex," Mike said. "That might be something different."

"What's the big deal about having sex in a helicopter?" Sue asked. "Other than being a little uncomfortable and cramped. You might as well do it in a broom closet."

I started laughing.

Sue playfully slapped my arm. "What's so funny?"

I looked at Mike. "You want to explain, buddy?"

Gina looked as confused as Sue.

"You mean you girls never heard of helicopter sex?" Mike asked.

Gina and Sue looked at each other and shook their heads.

Mike rubbed his hand over his mouth.

"Come on, Mike," Gina said. "Out with it."

"Well, the guy's on the bottom and the girl's on top and the guy grabs the girl's legs and twirls her around."

"There's no way in hell you're going to grab my legs like they're helicopter blades and twirl me around. I'd fall off and you'd lose your penis," Gina said.

We all laughed and got dirty stares from diners at nearby tables. Gina had said "penis" just a little too loudly.

Sue

"So anyone else have something you've never done but want to try?" I asked.

"A threesome might be good," Tom said.

I slapped Tom's arm.

"I was talking golf."

"Sure you were."

"I'd like to learn how to scuba dive," Gina said. "But I have a real fear of being down deep in the ocean and my air running out."

"Speaking of the ocean, sex in the ocean would be good," Mike said. "A little salty but good."

"Ocean sex isn't all it's cracked up to be," I said.

"How would you know?" asked Tom.

"Well, let's just say that salt isn't one of Vagina's friends—and neither is sand."

"That's what you have a big blanket for," Tom said.

"Yeah, but you gotta stay on the blanket," I winked.

"I'm with Sue on this one," Gina said. "Just thinking about all of the different organisms in the ocean getting inside of me. Yuck! I'd be afraid of getting some kind of infection. And pool sex isn't much better. The chlorine isn't exactly good for the vagina either."

"If you ask me, probably the best water sex is in the shower—as long as you don't slip," I said.

"Yeah, wasn't it Cookie who slipped in the shower and bruised her tailbone?" Gina asked.

I nodded. "And she went out and bought some anti-skid stickers to put on the bottom."

Mike and Tom shook their heads.

"Well, well. We're learning a lot from these girls tonight, aren't we, Tom?"

Tom laughed. "Yeah. And I'm thinking I need to buy some anti-skid stickers on the way home."

I playfully nudged Tom. "This is one horny table."

Thank God the waiter arrived or I think we would've had to take turns slipping inside a nearby closet for a quickie.

Chapter 6

Tom

I took Sue's arm and helped her into the car. It doesn't take much booze to get her drunk. We always teased her about it in high school. Some things never change. When she started to slur her words, I knew it was time to head home.

Gina laughed. "Sure you don't need any help?"

I shook my head. "Chloe's still at her dad's, and Sue was planning on spending the night at my house. I'll make sure she drinks some water before going to bed."

"I'd forgotten how little it takes her to get drunk." Mike laughed.

"Well, she had a ball," Gina said. "But she might feel like crap in the morning."

I followed Gina and Mike out of the parking lot, and when I looked over at Sue she was slouched against the car door, sound asleep. I listened to her putt-putt snore on the way home. It was kind of funny, actually. I kept thinking how mortified she'd be if she knew she snored.

Dinner with Gina and Mike was great. I hadn't laughed so hard in all my life. I kept playing the conversations over in my mind. Like the conversation about what girls talk about.

"You know," Sue had said. "Sex. Good sex. Bad sex. Penis size."

"You actually talk about penis size?" I asked.

"Yeah," Sue said. "And vibrators. "Cookie says a vibrator is the only remote she and her ex didn't fight over."

We all laughed. Cookie was a character, and listening to Sue describe Cookie asking the girls at a recent luncheon if they thought a finger in the butt hole during a blow job was a good idea made my sides hurt from laughing. Sue gets really loose when she drinks and things that she normally wouldn't say just sort of pop out. I like that silly side of her.

Then Gina brought up periods, and how girls spend a lot of time talking about them.

"You mean Blowjob Week." Mike laughed.

Gina smacked his arm. "Well, I'm sure if you were bleeding from your penis for a week every month it's *all* we'd hear about."

By the time I pulled into my garage, I think I'd laughed even harder the second time around just replaying the conversations in my mind.

∽

I carried Sue into the house and up to my bed. She started to stir when I laid her down. I debated whether to undress her or just put her in bed as she was. I took off her shoes and she cracked her eyes.

She moaned. "Aren't you going to join me?"

"Are you sure you're feeling up to it?" I asked.

She started taking off her dress. "Got any peppermint schnapps?"

"I'm not sure you should have anything more to drink."

She ran her tongue over her lips and pointed her finger at me. "It's not for me; it's for you."

I had no idea what she wanted to do with the peppermint schnapps. But by this time, my groin was aching to find out.

Sue

I knew I was a little tipsy. Still, I was as horny as hell. Not only does alcohol make me playful, our dinner conversation didn't help. Besides, I'd read something in a women's magazine, and I was dying to try it. Tonight seemed like a good night, especially since I'd let my inhibitions down.

I smelled my armpits. Still smelled like vanilla lavender. I grabbed by purse, which Tom had thrown on the bed when he carried me upstairs, and yanked out a small vial of perfume. I put a dab behind each ear. I didn't want to overpower him with scent.

By the time Tom returned, I was completely undressed and waiting on top of the sheets.

Tom held up a bottle of peppermint schnapps and a glass of water. "Found the schnapps, but first drink this water."

"Do I have to?" I pouted.

"If you want the schnapps you do."

Reluctantly, I took the glass of water.

"Drink it all," Tom said. "Not just a sip."

I managed to drink the entire glass and set it on the nightstand.

I watched as Tom unbuttoned his white shirt and slid out of it. Then he unbuckled his belt and dropped his pants.

I laid back and opened the bottle of schnapps. "Pour this in my belly button and then sip it."

I tried to keep still as Tom filled my navel with the schnapps. Then he sat the bottle on the nightstand and leaned down to sip it. That magazine article was right. He was driving me crazy with desire. When he kissed my breasts and then blew on the spots he kissed with his peppermint-tinged lips, I thought I would go insane.

I lifted his head. "Kiss me." And when our mouths found each other, I could taste the peppermint on his tongue.

"I'm going to sip some more," he said.

I could feel my desire for him building as he filled my belly button and sipped the schnapps once again. The things he was doing to me felt incredible, and I couldn't take it anymore.

"Please," I begged. "I need you."

And when he slid inside me my whole world turned upside down.

Tom

I filled the coffee maker with water. Last night was full of firsts. I'd never drunk peppermint schnapps out of anyone's belly button or rolled around in bed so passionately that I fell out of it. It sounds more painful than it was. We ended up on the floor and, except for some minor carpet burns, it was the best sex I'd ever had.

I'd decided to let Sue sleep in. I figured she was probably feeling pretty rough. I knew she had to be home after lunch because Chloe's dad was dropping her off at 2. I was heading out of town in the morning for a conference, so I wasn't going to see Sue until next Friday. After last night, maybe that was a good thing. I never thought I'd say this, but it's not as easy for me to hit the sex replay button as when I was younger. The replay button needed a rest.

I heard her moans before I saw her. Sue walked into the kitchen wearing my dress shirt from last night. Her hair was a tangled nest, but she still looked damn sexy.

Sue rubbed her head. "Do I look as bad as I feel?"

I smiled. "You look great."

"Yeah, right. Don't lie."

"Okay, you look a little rough, but you still look sexy."

Sue smiled. "My head is killing me. How much did I drink last night, anyway?"

I filled up a mug with coffee and handed it to her. "Don't you remember?"

"Kind of lost count after the second bottle of champagne. But I didn't forget what happened when we got back here."

I smiled. "You were great." I wrapped my arms around her and kissed the top of her head. "What do you want to eat?"

"Anything. I need to take something for this headache, but I don't want to take it on an empty stomach."

"How about an egg sandwich?"

Sue sipped her coffee. "An egg sandwich would be perfect."

Sue

I watched as Tom flipped the egg in the cast iron frying pan. "There's something else I remember from last night."

"Oh yeah," Tom said. "You mean how great of a lover I am?"

"Well, that's true. But I'm talking about your ex."

"Ah, Rachel. Figured we'd have to have that conversation sooner or later."

Tom handed me my egg sandwich. "Mustard or ketchup?"

"Mustard."

Tom sat the mustard and some fresh strawberries on the table.

"This looks delicious," I told him. "Thank you."

After refilling his coffee mug, he sat across from me. He took a deep breath. "Okay, about Rachel. Yes, we were engaged. And, yes, I called it off about a month before the wedding. I just couldn't go through with it."

"Did you love her?"

"In the beginning, yes. But definitely not at the end. I should've called it quits long before I did, but I felt stuck. And I felt like a jerk for letting it go on like I did. But God, there was just no way I wanted to grow old with her. And, honestly, I can't believe I even got with her in the first place. She's not my type at all."

I sipped my coffee. "So how did you meet, anyway?"

Tom ran his fingers through his hair. "Her dad and I are on the YMCA board. He introduced me to her at a charity event. Anyway, when I broke it off, Rachel went berserk. Threw all of my stuff out of her apartment window, started calling me all hours of the night."

"So she didn't take it well?"

"That's putting it mildly. She was more pissed than a bull charging a waving flag. I offered to reimburse her parents for the wedding deposits, but Rachel said she wasn't some kind of charity case, and that I could stick my money up my ass. I was just glad the whole thing was over. It's a part of my past that I'm not too proud of."

"Well, from the look on Rachel's face last night, I'd say she's still carrying the torch for you."

"She might be carrying it, but it hasn't been lit for a long time. I'm sorry I hadn't mentioned the engagement and near-wedding before. I guess it's just not something I like talking about. But I would've eventually."

I could feel the sting in my eyes, and I was sure they were glassy. "You can't keep things from me, Tom. Not something that important."

"I'm sorry, Sue. Honestly, I would've told you. I know after what happened with Steve you probably have trust issues. Guess I just wasn't thinking about that. I should have."

"Well, there is a way you could make it up to me." I bit my bottom lip seductively.

"Name it."

"How about some shower sex?"

Tom smiled. "I thought you'd never ask. But just so you know, I don't have any anti-skid stickers to put on the floor."

"Somehow I think we'll manage," I said, running up the stairs as fast as I could.

Chapter 7

Tom

Klondike and I were walking through the park when we ran into Judy. Judy was with Gina's mom when Betty died unexpectedly in New York. I used to see them walking in the park nearly every day. Now, Judy walks alone. I feel sorry for her.

She stopped and waited for me to catch up. "Hi, Tom. How's everything?"

"Not bad. How about you?"

"Really missing Betty."

I nodded. We started walking together. "Guess you heard I'm seeing Sue."

Judy smiled. "Yes, Gina stopped by and updated me on all of the news. I'm happy for both of you."

"Guess you're excited about Gina moving back home, huh?"

Judy nodded. "I am, but I just hope she knows what she's doing. She's spent years building her career, and to walk away from that to start over here, well, I can only say one thing, she must really love Mike."

"I don't think she ever stopped." I wasn't sure how much Gina had told Judy. Like if she knew about the rape. And if Gina hadn't, then I didn't want to be the one to tell her.

"Guess all that praying we did for good sperm for Gina worked out," Judy laughed. "Just not in the way we thought it would."

I scratched my head. I had no idea what Judy was talking about. I guess she noticed my puzzled look because she explained.

"Betty had all of us at card club praying that Gina got good sperm. That's when she was going to get pregnant with donor sperm from a sperm bank. Well, she got good sperm. At least I think Mike's got good sperm. But it didn't come from the donor whose profile she'd chosen from the bank registry."

I laughed. "Yeah, no need for donor sperm now."

"Do you want kids?" Judy asked.

One thing I've learned about older people is that they ask very personal questions no one my age would. Just like this question. It's a pretty damn personal one. And if I'd been younger, I would've been embarrassed to answer. But now? What the heck.

"Well, to be honest, Judy, I would've loved to have had kids. Truth is, it's not in the cards for me. Chances are slim that it would ever happen. I had testicular cancer."

Judy's jaw dropped. "I'm sorry, Tom. I had no idea. Me and my big mouth."

I held up my hand. "No, seriously. Don't worry about it. Hey, I'm alive, aren't I? It didn't kill me."

I think Judy was glad we were near the turn-off to her car.

"This is my stop," she said. "I'll see you and Klondike again, I'm sure."

Klondike and I continued down the stony path. I passed a group of kids playing in the field, and it made me smile. I always thought there'd be a little me running around. And then when the chances grew slim, I set that dream aside. But I couldn't help wondering what my kid would look like if Sue was the mother. Damn, I think we'd make some good looking kids.

Sue

I was upstairs putting wash away when I heard Gina call from the bottom of the steps. She was headed back to Florida and wanted to check in before leaving for the airport.

"I'm in my bedroom!" I yelled.

Gina walked in and gave me a hug. "You feeling okay?"

"It was a little rough this morning, but I'm feeling better now."

I grabbed my sheets to put on the bed, and Gina went to the opposite side to help.

"I figured. You were pretty toasted last night. Course, you don't need much," she laughed.

I threw the sheet on top of the bed, and Gina pulled it toward her. "Just tell me that I didn't totally embarrass myself."

"No, nothing to be worried about," said Gina, grabbing the comforter off the floor. "Besides, you were having a great time, and you deserve to have a great time. Tom is so in love with you."

I pulled the comforter toward me. "You think?"

"Definitely."

Gina and I sat on the bed.

"Omigod," I squirmed. "I gotta tell you this before Chloe comes home. So you know that magazine article I told you about?"

"You mean the one about the sexy stuff you can do with your man?"

I nodded. "Yeah, that one. Well, we did the peppermint schnapps thing last night."

Gina's eyes widened. "Was it good?"

"Better than good. Tom sipped the schnapps from my belly button and then kissed my breasts and blew on the spots he kissed. Christ, I'm getting horny just thinking about it."

Gina laughed. "Man, you got it bad."

"Jesus, Gina. I had no idea sex could be this good. The more I'm with Tom the more I realize what a lousy lay Steve was."

Gina laughed. "Well, since you're kissing and telling, I have to tell you about dessert."

I nodded.

"Last night after we got home, Mike tells me that we're going to have dessert in bed. And I'm thinking that's kind of weird because he's got this hang-up about eating in bed. I think it goes back to when he was a kid and his mom never let him eat in bed. Something about crumbs and ants and, anyway. So we go to bed and we get undressed and he takes this box of chocolate truffles that he apparently bought earlier and stashed in his nightstand drawer. And, oh my God, just thinking about it gets me excited. He tells me that we're going to eat the truffle together and he places the truffle into his mouth and motions for me. We kissed to share it. And the truffle just melted and our tongues were chocolaty and it was so freakin' hot."

I rubbed my hands together. "Oh. My. God. I have to try that."

"I swear we're worse than when we were seventeen," Gina said.

"Way worse."

"So did you talk about his ex?" Gina asked.

"Yes. He told me about the engagement and how he called it off a month before the wedding. Sounds like it was a lot of drama."

"Well, she didn't look like someone I'd want to cross. Definite bedroom eyes that could turn serpent in a second."

"So when do you think you'll be back?" I asked Gina.

"Not for a couple of weeks. I have that horrific college rape case I need to work on. But I have all of the house contractors lined up, and they should begin renovations sometime next week. I gave them your number and Mike's. I have a lot to figure out and a lot to do."

"Well, whatever you need me to do from here, just let me know."

Gina hugged me. "Thanks. You've done so much already."

We heard Chloe come in the back door and rushed downstairs to see her.

Tom

When Klondike and I got back from the park, he headed for the sofa. I ran upstairs to shower, and when I lifted the toilet seat to pee there was a Post-it note stuck to the underside.

Have a fabulous trip. I miss you already, Sue

I pulled off the note and stuck it on the wall. Only Sue would think to put a Post-it note on the underside of a toilet seat! God, she makes me smile.

It reminded me of our toilet paper conversation earlier. Sue went to the bathroom and laughingly complained that the toilet paper roll was on wrong. I had it overhang and she thought it should be under hang. Anyway, that led back to our toilet seat up or down conversation we had days earlier when I left the seat up and she nearly fell in. I smiled remembering it.

"Look," she had said. "You have to learn to put the toilet seat down. I got a wet ass!"

I laughed. "You didn't look before you sat?"

"No, but that's beside the point. I shouldn't have to look because the seat should always be down."

I smiled. "Look. I'm a guy. And I'm used to living alone. So, naturally I keep the seat up."

Sue gave me her pouty lips. "Well, will you try to remember to put it down?"

"I'll try to remember."

I jumped in the shower and as I remembered the great shower sex we had that morning, I remembered that I needed to get some of those anti-skid stickers. It can get pretty slippery if there's nothing to hold onto and things get pretty fast. And they always seem to get that way with Sue.

༄

Klondike watched as I packed my suitcase. Sue had volunteered to watch him while I was away. She said Chloe would love having him for the week, and I was happy I didn't have to board him. He hates it at the kennel. And when I pick him up, he's always hoarse for a day or two. I have a feeling he barks non-stop.

I was going to drop him off later tonight on my way to the airport. I had a late flight.

I figured we'd get some dinner, watch some TV, and head over to Sue's about eight.

Sue

Chloe heaved her backpack onto the table. "Hi, Mom. Aunt Gina. How was your weekend?"

I hugged Chloe and kissed her cheek. "Great, but I missed you."

Gina hugged Chloe, too. "I wish I could stay, but I have to get to the airport. I'll see you girls in a couple of weeks. When's Tom bringing Klondike over?"

"Klondike's coming?" Chloe asked.

"Actually, he's spending the week. Tom has a conference, and I offered to keep Klondike so he wouldn't have to go to the kennel."

Chloe did a fist pump. "Awesome."

"Tom's dropping him off around eight."

Gina turned toward the door. "Well, have a great week. Call me if anything comes up."

"Don't worry about the house," I yelled after her. "I'll check on the contractors."

⌒ ⌒

I could tell by the way Chloe chewed her bottom lip and wrung her hands that she wanted to talk to me about something. I sat down at the table across from her. "What's on your mind, Chloe?"

"Why do you think something's on my mind?"

"Because I'm your mother, and I know these things. So let's have it."

Chloe sat up straight. "Well, there is something I wanted to talk to you about. It's, uh... well, Rob. Rob asked me out, and I really, really, really want to go."

I took a deep breath. I wasn't surprised. I knew by the way he was hanging around it was only a matter of time. But I wasn't ready to deal with this quite yet. "But you're only 14. He's 17. That's three years older, in case you didn't count."

"He just turned 17, so it's really only two years older," Chloe said. "Besides, you and dad were six years apart."

"True, we were. But six years' difference when you're 23 is different than being six years apart—or two—when you're fourteen. And besides, he has a car."

"Duh, yeah, Mom. How else would we go out on a date if he didn't have a car?"

"I don't know, Chloe," I said. "I don't like cars. Things can happen in a car."

"Mom! Things can happen anywhere. Besides, you dated when you were fourteen, so why can't I?"

"That's beside the point."

"No, it's not, Mom. You dated when you were 14, and you turned out just fine."

"But I wish I would've waited to date for a couple of years. Look, Chloe, things can happen fast at your age."

"You're talking about sex."

I could feel my face warm up. "Yes, as a matter of fact I am."

"Look, Mom. It's not like I don't know about the birds and the bees. Besides, I'm not going to have sex until I'm married."

I smiled. "You say that now, but in the heat of the moment, that can get tossed out the window pretty fast. I just think you should wait. At least another year."

Chloe pushed out her chair and stood up. "You and Dad just don't understand. You're ruining my life."

"Oh, so you already asked your dad?"

"Yes. And he said no. Said he was going to start a DADD group."

"What's that?"

"Dads Against Daughters Dating."

I laughed a little.

"Don't laugh. He told me he didn't want me to date until I was at least 16."

"Well, maybe that's not a bad idea."

"I'm the only one of my friends who isn't allowed to date. Do you know how uncool that makes me?"

"What happened to 'The Nerds Rule'?"

Chloe crossed her arms. "That was so yesterday, Mom. I'm tired of being a nerd. For once in my life I want to be one of the cool kids."

Chloe grabbed her backpack and stumped upstairs. I heard her door slam and thought about going after her, but decided instead to let her go. She needed time to cool off. Maybe in a couple of hours we could talk, but I knew my daughter and talking now would only make things worse. She might have her dad's looks, but she has my stubbornness.

Chapter 8

Tom

I found Klondike asleep on the couch. "Come on, boy. Time to go."

His ears shot up.

"I'm taking you to Sue's house."

Klondike barked then leapt off the couch and ran to the door. I had a feeling he was as fond of Sue as I was.

Driving to Sue's house, I thought about how much I was going to miss her. We hadn't said the L word yet, but it was on the tip of my tongue. I thought about saying it last night. I really wanted to. It's how I feel. But I was worried that if I said it too soon, Sue would get scared and pull away. And the last thing I wanted was for Sue to withdraw. Having her in my life was the best thing that's ever happened to me.

After Rachel, I thought I'd spend my life alone. But now, I'm not so sure. When I saw Sue at the reunion, all of the old feelings I had for her in high school came racing back. Truth was, I'd always had a thing for her. Once, when she was in between boyfriends, I'd gotten up the courage to ask her out. I practiced and practiced what I was going to say. And the day I got the nerve to actually do it was the day John asked her out. I remember being so pissed because I knew he didn't like her as much as I did. No one did. And no one knew how much I liked her but Mike. I can remember his words as if he'd spoken them yesterday. "Told you to move faster, Tom. You had your opening, and you blew it."

Mike was right. And now that I had an opening some 20 years later, I wasn't going to blow it again. I wanted her in my life, and I planned to keep her there.

Sue

I heard the doorbell ring and Klondike bark. "Chloe," I yelled. "Klondike's here."

Chloe bolted from her bedroom and headed for the front door. "Can I take him for a walk?"

Tom smiled and handed her the leash.

Tom and I watched Chloe and Klondike head down the sidewalk. "That's the first she's been out of her room all day. We had an argument, and she's been holed up in there."

"I didn't think you two argued," said Tom, following me into the living room.

"We don't often. But I'm just not ready to let her date. Neither is her dad. Chloe wants to go out with the boy down the street. He's seventeen. She's fourteen."

Tom held up his hand. "Say no more."

"See, you're thinking the same thing I am."

"I just remember being 17. Of course, I wasn't one of the lucky ones who had a girlfriend. The girl I wanted was taken."

I playfully slapped his arm, and he pulled me in for a kiss.

"It's true," he said. "You always had a boyfriend. There was a window of opportunity in the winter of our junior year, but then John swooped in before I got up the nerve to ask you out."

I laughed. "Window of opportunity, huh? You make it sound like I entertained a revolving door of guys. "

"Whatever happened to John, anyway?" Tom asked.

"I lost touch after high school. Remember, he was a year older and went into the Army. I think he might have decided to make a career out of it. I'm pretty sure he never moved back."

Tom looked at his watch. "I should get going."

He handed me a piece of paper. "Here's all the information in case you need to reach me. I'm going to miss you." He pulled me closer, and our lips found one another.

"I wish we could have a repeat of the shower sex we had this morning right now," I whispered in his ear.

"Me, too," he said. "But that'll give us something to look forward to when I return."

"And when will that be?"

"I should be home by 8 Friday night."

I playfully grabbed his crotch and winked. "I'll be waiting for you in your bed."

"What, Chloe's not going to be home?"

I shook my head. "She's staying overnight at her best friend's for a birthday sleepover."

"In that case, I'll *really* have something to look forward to."

We kissed a long time before Tom pulled himself away and headed to his car. I was really falling for him. I almost told him I loved him. It was right then that I decided I'd tell him Friday night. And I couldn't wait!

Tom

The entire time I was driving to the airport, I couldn't stop thinking about Sue. And to think I almost didn't go to my high school reunion. It was only because Mike and a few of the other guys badgered me so much that I even went. I was sort of embarrassed that I didn't have a date, but then Mike told me he didn't either, and we could hang out together. Never expected I'd end up sitting with the one girl from high school who I always wanted to date but never had the chance to.

Because it was Sunday night, the traffic was light on the Interstate, and I arrived at the airport sooner than I'd expected. Security wasn't too bad either, and by the time I sat down at the gate, I had time to spare. So, I called Sue.

"You're there already?" she asked when she heard my voice.

"Yeah. Traffic wasn't bad, and the airport is pretty empty. How's Klondike?"

"He's fine. He hasn't left Chloe's side since he came. I think he found a new best friend."

I laughed. "He might not want to come home after spending the week."

"Well, I'm sure Chloe would keep him."

"What about you?" I asked.

Sue laughed. "I'd rather keep his dad."

I chuckled. "Sue..." It was on the tip of my tongue and I wanted to say it. But I wanted to tell her that I loved her face to face. I wanted to look into her eyes so she could see that I meant it.

"What?" Sue asked.

"Nothing. They just called for the first passengers. I'll call tomorrow. Probably won't be until 8 or so."

"Okay. Have a safe trip and sleep well."

"I'd sleep better if you were beside me."

"I'd sleep better, too. Remember," she whispered. "Shower sex Friday."

I hung up the phone and smiled. I was one lucky guy.

Sue

I crawled into bed and reached for one of my books on the nightstand. I had several stacked next to the phone and switched among them depending on my mood. Tonight, I was in the mood for some romance.

Thoughts of Rachel crept into my mind. I mean, the girl was gorgeous. I wondered what Tom saw in me. She had everything I didn't. Legs that went on forever. Boobs that, even if they weren't completely real, beckoned like a hooker looking to score.

Tom had told me that no matter how much guys talk about asses and boobs, it's personality that's most important. I'm sure he's right, but great asses and boobs to die for can't hurt.

I cupped my breast with my hand. One handful. That's all. It would take a front-end loader to hold Rachel's.

Thinking back over the last couple of months, I realized how empty my life had been. It's hard to miss something you never had. And even when Steve and I were together, it was never like it is with Tom. I didn't know it was possible for a guy to make me feel so beautiful, so wanted.

He even kissed the scars on my knees that I've always been self-conscious about. He told me that the scars were part of me, that they helped tell my life story. Okay. Come on now. What kind of guy says stuff like that? Seriously. This is the first one I've ever come across who finds beauty in imperfection. It's one of the things I love most about him.

Tom

The week dragged on like the day before vacation. You can't wait for it to end so you can unwind and relax. The conference was okay, but I found myself zoning out during the sessions and thinking about Sue a lot. I called every day and was glad to hear that Klondike didn't seem to miss me at all. By the time Friday rolled around, I couldn't wait to get home. Sue told me that after dropping Chloe off at her friend's, she'd bring Klondike over and stay with him until I got home. She hinted at a special welcome home.

The entire drive home, all I could think about was having shower sex. Seeing Sue naked in the shower, dripping wet. Damn! I heard a siren and looked in my rear view mirror and saw a whirl of flashing lights. A cop was on my tail. I pulled over. Turned out I was going 85 in a 65 zone. It sure as hell didn't feel like it.

The last time I got a speeding ticket I was 17, trying to make it home before my junior license curfew.

The officer waddled up to my window. His gut jutted out over his belt. *Where do they find these officers*, I wondered.

"What were you thinking going so fast?" the officer asked.

"Shower sex," I said.

He spread his feet apart so he could lower his head and look me in the eye. He sniffed and narrowed his eyes. "What did you say?"

"I need to go slower, I guess," I said, realizing this guy had zero sense of humor.

"You're darn right you need to go slower, son. A lot slower."

He wrote out the ticket, lectured some more, and I was finally on my way, a good half hour behind schedule. I was going to call Sue and tell her I'd be late, but my cell phone was dead.

Sue

I dropped Chloe off at her girlfriend's, and Klondike whimpered the entire fifteen-minute drive to his house.

I parked along the street, behind a car I didn't recognize. I opened the back door and Klondike bolted in, running from room to room as if he were looking for something or someone.

"It's about time you got..."

I turned around. My mouth dropped to the floor—and so did my heart. There was Rachel in eight-inch fuck me spike heels, wearing a lacy thong and heart-shaped nipple covers with tassels.

She put her hand to her heart. "Oh. It's you. I was expecting Tom." She licked her lips like a bar room tramp.

I could feel my face turning red. I pulled back my lips and bared my teeth. "What the fuck are you doing here?"

"Me?" she asked, her little nipple tassels jiggling. "I was going to ask you the same thing."

All I could think about was getting away from her, away from this house. It was like Steve all over again. My heart was breaking, and I couldn't stop the tears from coming. I ran to my car as fast as I could and took off.

Chapter 9

Tom

When I got home, the house was dark. I smiled, thinking about Sue waiting for me upstairs.

Klondike knows the sound of my car, and he was waiting for me just inside the back door. I gave him a big hug and a quick belly rub and went up to Sue. I looked over at the bed. Sue was completely under the covers. I figured she was playing possum. So I got naked and crawled in next to her. When I reach around her to pull her over, I realized that it wasn't Sue.

"Jesus fuckin' Christ, Rachel," I yelled, jumping out of bed. "What the fuck are you doing here?" I pulled on my jeans and shirt.

She uncovered herself. "Oh come on now, Tiger. Is that anyway to greet an old flame—one you were going to marry?"

"Jesus, no. No. Klondike's here. Which means Sue was here. Did Sue see you?"

Rachel slid out of bed and walked toward me. "You mean that little mouse of a girl you've been playing with? Of course she saw me. I thought it was you coming home. Imagine my surprise when it was Little Miss Debbie Cakes. She is a little doll, but not near enough woman for you." She shook her tits so her tassels swayed.

"Get the fuck out of my house or I'll rip those tassels off your tits. And if you ever pull another stunt like this, I'll file harassment charges. Now get out!"

"My, my, my. Such a bad temper. What happened to my pussycat of a man?"

"He turned into a tiger when he learned what a real woman was all about."

Sue

I wasn't sure where I was going. The only thing I knew is that I had to get away from Tom's house and that slut as fast as I could.

The scene played over and over in my mind. Rachel, thinking I was Tom, walking into the kitchen. Rachel, wearing that sexy get-up, looking like she was ready to perform at a strip club. She obviously had a key to Tom's place. Why would she still have the key? Maybe they did get together. Maybe Tom still felt something for her. After all, they were engaged, and he didn't tell me about that. My head was full of mixed thoughts. I was trying to make sense of the scene and what it might have meant.

My heart physically hurt. Tears soaked my face. Damn! I was mad at myself for allowing my heart to be broken again. I swore I'd never let it happen, never fall in love with a guy and let him have this power over me. But I thought Tom was different. I thought I could trust him. I thought, even though he didn't say it, that he loved me. I knew I loved him. And look what it got me- a woman with tassel tits.

I wasn't sure where to go, but I knew I needed to be alone. So I just drove, taking roads I'd never been on before. It was only when I realized my gas tank was on E that I pulled into a convenience store to fill up. I checked my cell phone and saw Tom had called, but he was the last person I wanted to talk to or see. I turned off my phone, not wanting to be bothered the rest of the night.

After I filled my gas tank, I headed home. I needed to talk with Gina, and I didn't want to be driving while I did that. I was too afraid I'd lose it and wreck the car. I had enough problems without doing something stupid like that, so I went home, a pile of wet tissues accumulating on the seat next to me.

Tom

"How'd you get my key anyway?" I shouted to Rachel as she got dressed.

"You never took it back. When I saw you with Little Miss Debbie Cakes I figured I needed to remind you of what you had given up. And for her? Christ, she looks like a damn doll. I figured that sooner or later you'd realize what you lost."

Rachel pulled the key out of her purse and threw it on the bed. "I hope you have a miserable life."

I watched her speed away and made a mental note to have the locks changed, just in case the bitch had made a copy of the key.

I tried calling Sue on her cell phone, but she wasn't picking up. I took a shot at calling her landline, but she wasn't answering that, either.

Klondike whimpered. "I know, boy. This is one fucked-up mess."

I figured the first person Sue would call would be Gina, but I didn't have Gina's cell phone number. So, I called Mike.

"Christ, you're never going to believe what Rachel just did," I told Mike.

I gave him the cliff notes and asked if he had heard from Gina.

"We just talked, and she didn't say anything," Mike said. "So I'm sure Sue didn't call her—yet."

"Can you give me Gina's number? I want to call her and explain. Just in case she hears from Sue. I want to make sure Gina knows what went down."

I wrote down Gina's number and called her right away. She was working at home.

I spewed out the entire ugly story. There was silence on the other end.

"Gina! Say something!"

"I'm speechless that Rachel would do such a thing. And angry as hell. I can't imagine what went through Sue's mind. It was probably Steve all over again. You know what happened there, right?"

"Yes. She came home and found him in bed with their neighbor."

"And after that, Sue pretty much swore off men," Gina said. "But you changed that. When you guys reconnected at the reunion, it was like her whole outlook on men changed. I could see it. She had hope. I think she loves you, Tom. I really do. And just when she allowed herself to feel that way again, Rachel screws it all up."

"Believe me, I know. It makes me sick."

"Look, I'm going to try to call her," Gina said. "Maybe when she sees it's me, she'll pick up."

"Will you call me if she does?"

"Yes. If I'm able to reach her and talk to her, I'll let you know. But that doesn't mean I'll be able to get her to talk to you. That has to be her decision."

"I know. But it's worth a shot. And Gina, I hadn't told Sue this. Fact is I was planning to tonight. I'd been feeling like this for a while. But when I told Sue, I wanted to be looking right into her eyes. I love her, Gina. And I was hoping she loved me, too."

Sue

When I got home, there were messages on the answering machine. I really didn't want to hear Tom's voice, but I didn't want to miss a call from Chloe.

I walked over to the counter and pushed the button.

"Sue. It's Tom. Don't hang up. Please. I'm sorry. I had no idea Rachel would pull a stunt like that. Call me as soon as you get this message. Please."

I listened to the message over and over. Tom seemed sincere. Still, I didn't want to deal with him right now. I had to think. And call Gina. I turned on my cell phone and saw missed calls from Tom and Gina. I dialed Gina right away.

"I've been trying to reach you," Gina said. "Tom called and told me what happened. He's worried about you."

I couldn't hold back the tears. They came like a driving rain, blinding me in a liquid fog. "Did he tell you what happened? That Rachel was there? It was awful, Gina. God! She thought I was Tom, and she strutted into the kitchen in her fuck-me heels wearing lingerie that made her look like a hooker hoping to score. Christ, she even wore nipple covers with tassels. Tassels, Gina. She was obviously ready to get it on in a big way."

I exploded like a shaken soda bottle when it's opened. Every time Gina tried to inject a comment, my words just plowed right over hers.

"And another thing, she had to have a key to get in. Why in the hell would she have a key if Tom didn't want her to?"

"Sue," Gina said. "Please. Try to calm down."

"I can't calm down. I was going to tell him that I loved him tonight, Gina. I was actually going to fall for this love shit again. I'm so stupid. Stupid. Stupid. Stupid."

"You're not stupid," Gina said. "And you're not thinking straight."

"You're not taking his side, are you?"

"I'm not taking anyone's side. I just want you to think. Tom knew you were going to be at his house when he got home, right?"

"Yes, the plan was for me to bring Klondike over and then wait for him. And I had it all planned out. It was going to be a romantic evening. I even shaved twice! I was going to wait for him in bed. I even bought some sexy lingerie. Of course, mine didn't have tassels. He probably likes tassels."

"Sue!"

"What? He probably does. Well, screw him. I threw the lingerie in the trash when I stopped to fill up the gas tank. We were going to have shower sex, Gina. Shower sex. Christ, I'm so dumb. Dumb! Dumb! Dumb!"

"Sue," Gina shouted. "Listen. Do you really think Tom would've invited Rachel over if he knew you were going to be there?"

"Maybe he wanted to do a threesome."

"Come on. You know Tom's not like that."

"No, I don't. I thought I knew what Tom was like but maybe I don't. Maybe you don't, either."

"One, Tom's not like that. Two, if he was, which he's not, he wouldn't have invited his ex and his girlfriend over at the same time. That would be suicide."

"So he's dumb."

"No, he's actually very smart, and you know it."

"I don't know, Gina. Stranger things have happened."

"Look," Gina said. "I want you to just think about it overnight. I really think if you think about it you'll see that Tom inviting Rachel over just doesn't make sense."

I finally sat down on the couch. "Maybe you're right. I just feel drained from crying so much. And I'm tired."

"I wish I was there," Gina said. "I'll call you tomorrow morning. We'll talk some more. I love you."

"I love you, too."

I hung up the phone and pulled the bottle of wine I had planned to share with Tom out of my overnight bag. I was going to drink and forget.

Tom

"Wow! Talk about causing a fire," Gina said. "Rachel caused an inferno."

"It's that bad, huh?" I asked.

"It's badder than bad. I tried to reason with her. I told her you would've never invited your ex and girlfriend over at the same time."

"Is that what she thinks? That I planned it?"

"Right now, Tom, she's so hurt and angry that she doesn't know what to believe. I think in the morning, when she's thinking more clearly, she'll see things differently."

"So you don't think I should go over and see her now, try to talk some sense into her? Get this whole thing straightened out?"

"No. Not tonight. Give her time, Tom. At least until tomorrow. I know Sue, and when she gets like this, you just have to let her go. It's like trying to stop a raging bull. She sees a waving flag even if there is none. Tomorrow, she'll see things differently."

I ran my fingers through my hair. "But what if she doesn't?"

"Well, I don't know. I hope she'll be able to see through Rachel. She told me all about her nipple covers with tassels."

"Christ, Gina. I can't believe Rachel did something like this. I guess when she saw Sue and me out the other night it must've really pissed her off. Rachel always said she hoped my life sucked. Guess she could tell from the way things looked that my life didn't exactly suck. So, she did what she could to fuck it up. Bitch."

"Well, hang in there, Tom. I told Sue I'd call her tomorrow."

"Will you call me afterward?"

"Yes. But after that, I'm not playing go-between. Sue already asked me if I was taking sides. I'm not. You're both my friends, but Sue is my best friend, and no matter what, I have to be there for her. Do you understand?"

"Yes. I just need to know that she's all right. And hope that in time, she'll talk to me and we can get this whole thing straightened out."

"I hope for that, too," Gina said. "By the way, I'd do something about the locks on your house."

"I already made that call," I told her. "The locksmith's coming tomorrow."

Chapter 10

Sue

I knew I shouldn't have downed the entire bottle of wine. I spent part of the night hugging the toilet, and I had a killer headache. Thank God I didn't have to pick up Chloe until noon so I could stay in bed.

I wish last night was a bad dream, that when I woke up everything I thought had happened was just my imagination and fear working overtime. But once I got my bearings, I knew that it wasn't. And I got angry all over again. Angry that Rachel was so damn beautiful. Angry that I was angry that Rachel looked so damn beautiful when I knew in my heart she was as cheap as those nipple covers with tassels she wore. Angry that Rachel had a key to Tom's place. Angry that Tom gave Rachel a key to his place. Angry. Angry. Angry. At the whole world. But mostly at myself for allowing even a smidgen of hope that I could find a man to spend the rest of my life with, one who wouldn't always be looking over my shoulder for something better, who accepted me for who I was and didn't try to make me into something I wasn't.

What is it about men? Are there no good ones left? I think Gina found the last good guy. Or, correction, she realized she had a great guy, one she was willing to change her whole life for. A guy has never loved me that much—ever!

Maybe there are those of us who aren't meant to have great guys. Maybe it's God's way of controlling the population or something. Hell, I don't know. All I know is that my heart still feels as broken as it did last night and for some reason, what happened with Tom bothers me more than I wish it did. I don't like what that tells me because I realize I loved him even more than I admitted to myself. And I don't want to love him. Not now. Not ever.

Tom

The locksmith came first thing in the morning. I had him change the locks and add deadbolts. I definitely didn't want a repeat of last night.

I sipped my coffee and tried to read the morning paper. I wanted to call Gina and check to see if she had talked to Sue, but I knew it was too early to call. Besides, Gina had said she'd call me. I was lousy as hell at being patient. I wanted to go over to Sue's and try to explain everything face to face.

I ran my fingers through my hair. Christ, I was tired. I tossed and turned the night before. Damn, I can't believe I ever loved Rachel, that I'd actually asked her to marry me. Was I that desperate? To be fair, it wasn't until the breakup that Rachel started acting so whacked out. Before, she was just a spoiled little brat who got everything she wanted. That's what I got tired of. Her sense of entitlement and me-first attitude. But I had no idea she had this nasty side to her, a side that was hell-bent on revenge and making my life miserable.

I thought after she started seeing the surgeon, whom I'd heard about from an acquaintance, that things would get better. She got the rich guy she wanted, and because he was older and established, she would be well cared for. She had no worries. I'm sure he spoiled Rachel just like her father had spoiled her.

I still got the occasional drunken call in the middle of the night, but she never, until yesterday, showed up at my house damn near naked.

I needed to get out of the house. I couldn't sit around any longer.

I reached down to pet Klondike. "Want to go to the park, boy?"

He barked and went to the door. Sometimes, I think Klondike understands me better than anyone.

I grabbed my keys off the counter and my cell phone, just in case Gina called while we were out.

Sue

I was about ready to jump in the shower when Chloe called.

"Hey, Mom. Mind if I spend another night at Robin's house?"

"Is it okay with her mom?"

"Yeah. She said she'd drop us off at the mall later. So can I?"

I sat back down on the bed. "I don't know. I've barely seen you this week."

"Please, Mom. Please. Please. Please."

I had to admit, being able to crawl back into bed was tempting. "Okay. What time do you want me to pick you up?"

"Mrs. Matthews said she'd drop me off on their way to church, unless I wanted to go with them, which I don't."

"Okay, then I'll see you tomorrow. Behave."

"Thanks, Mom. I love you."

"I love you, too."

No sooner had I crawled back under the covers when Gina called.

"How's my bestie this morning?" said Gina in a sickening sing-song voice.

"You're too happy. Stop it."

"Okay. How's this then?" In her best Eeyore voice, Gina said, "Good morning."

"That's too gloomy."

"I can't win with you. Too happy. Too gloomy. Ugh. So are you still pissed off?"

"Yes. Maybe even a little more than I was last night."

"How can that be?" Gina asked. "Time is supposed to make you less pissed, not more."

"I know. I know. But I kept thinking about the key and Rachel having the key and why Rachel had the key."

"So she had the key," Gina said.

"Well, don't you think it's odd she had the key? Like why didn't Tom get the key back?"

"Maybe he forgot she had it."

"Or maybe he wanted her to have it?"

"Why?"

"Maybe he was leaving the door open a crack," I said. "You know, figuratively speaking."

"That doesn't make sense," Gina said. "Look, Sues, you know I love you. That I'd do anything for you. But I really think you're mad at the wrong person. Be mad at Rachel. Hell, be furious with her. But not at Tom. I really don't think you're giving him a fair shake. You won't even listen to his explanation?"

"How do you know that?"

"Because I know he called you and you didn't return his call," Gina explained.

"Did he call you?" I asked.

"Of course he called me. I'm your best friend. He's worried about you."

"Well, you can tell him not to worry. I'm a big girl, and I'll be just fine."

"Are you going to talk to him? Answer the phone if he calls?"

"Gina, I know Tom is your friend. But I'm your *best* friend. And right now I'm hurting. You're probably right. What Rachel did wasn't his fault. But it happened, and it's made me think twice about our relationship. Do I really want to take the chance and love again? When I saw Rachel, all I could think about was when I found Steve screwing little Miss Pierced Nipples. And I don't want to go through that heartache again. Ever."

"What did you tell me about Mike?" Gina asked. "About second chances. Starting over. You should take your own advice."

"It was different between you and Mike. You two were torn apart by a horrible, horrible incident that no one knew about. You never stopped loving one another. I was just falling in love with Tom. Stopping it now means I won't get hurt."

"But sometimes, Sues, you have to take chances. Do you want to live the rest of your life alone?"

"I have Chloe."

"Yes, you have Chloe. Now. But one day she'll go off on her own, and you'll be by yourself. And that's fine if that's what you want. But I, better than anyone, know how lonely that can be."

"But I have you."

"Sure, and you'll always have me. But that's not the same as having a man who loves you and who you love. All I'm saying is think about it. Think about it before you close that door for good. I don't want you to get hurt, but I don't want you to miss out on growing old with a man who's loved you for a long time. So, if he calls, think about answering the phone."

"I'll think about it. Maybe you're right. Maybe I should at least listen to him. But even if I do, I'm not promising anything."

"Good, that's all I'm asking. Just listen to what Tom has to say. If you still feel the way you feel now, well, okay then."

"How'd you get so smart, anyway? I asked.

Gina laughed. "It was reading all those damn Snapple caps!"

Tom

Klondike and I passed the wooden picnic pavilion when my cell phone rang.

"Hi, Gina. How's Sue?"

I could tell by the somber tone of Gina's voice that things hadn't gone the way I'd hoped. I walked to a nearby bench and sat down.

"I think she's just going to need a little time," Gina said. "We talked a lot, and I think I got through to her, but she was so hurt by Steve, and seeing Rachel just took her back to that time."

"Christ, Gina. That was more than a decade ago."

"I know. But you should know better than anyone how something that happens in the past can stay with you a long time."

I knew what Gina was referring to. She was talking about the night she was raped by our math teacher and how she kept it a secret for twenty years. It destroyed her relationship with Mike. It's also what led her to become an attorney that prosecutes sex crimes.

"But she has to know I'd never hurt her. God, I love her," I said.

"I know that. But here's the thing, Tom. She's hung up on the key. Why Rachel had the key, why you hadn't gotten the key back from Rachel. Her mind is working overtime, and she can't stop focusing on the key."

"Well, she won't have to worry about that anymore because the locks have been changed. Plus I had the locksmith add deadbolts. To be honest, Gina, I'd forgotten all about Rachel having the key. But I'm also angry at Sue for thinking so little of me. I'm hurt that she isn't giving me the chance to explain. I thought she valued our relationship more than that."

Gina sighed. "She'll come around. Finding Rachel dressed like a whore in your home made her doubt things. I'm not saying she was right to have doubts, but I can understand, given her past, why."

I got up from the park bench and started walking Klondike again. "So what am I supposed to do?"

"Give her time."

"How much time?"

"I don't know. Maybe a day or two. I gave her a lot to think about, so my guess is she'll eventually give you a chance to explain."

"This isn't how I thought I'd be spending my weekend," I said.

"Well, if it makes you feel any better, I know it's not what Sue had planned either. But, and I know I'm going to sound like Suzy Sunshine, I really do believe that if things are meant to be, they will be. Mike and I are proof of that. It might've taken 20 years, but we're finally together."

"Christ, I hope I don't have to wait 20 years for Sue to come around."

"Me, too."

I hung up the phone and Klondike and I headed for the car. What I really wanted to do was go over to Sue's house and insist she listened to me. I was willing to take the chance she'd slam the door in my face. I could handle that. What I couldn't handle was losing her without a fight. I hated feeling as if she was slipping through my fingers, and I was powerless to do anything about it.

I wanted to tell her that she was the best thing that's ever happened to me, and that I didn't plan on giving up on us.

Chapter 11

Sue

I jumped in the shower after I finished talking with Gina. As much as I hated to admit it, she made some good points. If I really stopped and thought about it rationally, Tom inviting Rachel over knowing that I'd be waiting for him didn't make any sense, unless he was a mean-spirited son of a bitch, and I knew in my heart he wasn't.

Truth was, it was probably just damn coincidence that Rachel was there when I showed up. She probably didn't even know Tom was out of town. How could she? She probably checked the house, discovered he wasn't home, and set her plan in motion. Maybe she expected just him to come home. Or maybe she thought we'd come home to find her. My guess is that she never imagined I'd be coming to Tom's alone. I'm sure she felt like she won the door prize when I showed up with Klondike.

I no sooner had dressed when Mom called.

"Suzy, it's Mom."

Mom still calls me Suzy and when she calls she always identifies herself. Kind of cracks me up. Like I don't know from her voice who's calling. "Hi, Mom."

"You didn't call me yesterday," Mom said.

I sat down on the edge of my bed. "Was I supposed to?"

"No, but you usually do. But you didn't so I was worried. Everything okay, Suzie Q?"

"Yes, Mom, everything's okay."

"Still seeing that nice boy? What's his name? Tim?"

"Tom, Mom. His name's Tom."

"Tim, Tom, it's the same except one letter. Maybe I should just call him T. That way it won't matter if I can't remember if it's an 'i' or an 'o.'"

I loved the way Mom thought. Sometimes her perspective of life made me laugh out loud.

"Anyway," Mom said. "I wanted to check to see if you were coming for Sunday dinner. Your sister is coming, and she's bringing her new boyfriend. I thought maybe John and T…"

"Her boyfriend's name is Jack, Mom. Not John."

"Whatever," she said. "Jack is a nickname for John, don't you know? Like people called John Kennedy Jack." She paused as if she was figuring out an easy way to remember Jack's name. "I thought it might be nice for J and T to meet," she finally said.

"I don't know, Mom."

"What do you mean, you don't know? You like this Tim, right?"

"Tom, Mom, it's Tom. And yes, I like him. But we sort of kind of had a fight."

"Oh for the love of God, girl. About what?"

I told Mom the vanilla version of finding Rachel at Tom's, which means I didn't go into details about Rachel's nipple covers with tassels.

"Sounds to me like that girl needs a good talkin' to," Mom said. "But I don't get why you're mad at T. What did he do?"

"It's more like what he didn't do," I explained. "Like he never got the key back."

"Good Lord, girl," Mom said. "You're the Queen of Forgetfulness. What about the time you kept forgetting to put lunch money in Chloe's school account and the poor girl couldn't buy lunch?"

"Did you have to bring that up, Mom, and make me feel like Lousy Mother of the Year all over again?"

"All I'm saying is that people forget things. Important things. Like putting lunch money in their daughter's account so the poor thing can eat and doesn't have to starve. So, what about dinner?"

"Chloe and I will be there. But I'm not sure about Tom. I thought maybe I'd talk to him tonight, try to clear things up."

"I know you rarely listen to me, Suzy, but I think that's a good idea. I didn't raise you to let some little floozy get the best of you. You should've sucker punched her."

"Mom!"

I finally got off the phone with Mom after listening to her tell me about the time she sucker punched a "floozy" at a school dance and gave her a bloody nose.

I figured I'd grab something to eat then go over to Tom's. I'd thought about calling, but I wanted to talk face to face.

Tom

I took Klondike home and decided to grab a bite before I headed over to Sue's. There wasn't a lot to eat in the house. Because I was out of town, I hadn't gone to the store. But I did find some eggs and fried up a few.

I was eating my last bite when Mike called. "How's it going?"

"Been better."

"Yeah, that Rachel's a real piece of work."

"Tell me about it. I really thought that when she started seeing that surgeon she'd leave me alone."

"Yeah," Mike said. "I remember the time she sent you the box of dead roses."

"And what about the time I found that nasty note on the windshield of my car and the air left out of my tires?"

"I'd forgotten about the flat tires," Mike said. "Well, you know what they say about a woman scorned."

"Yeah. I just hope she's had enough now. I threatened that if she comes near me again, she'll be hearing from my attorney."

"And I just happen to know a very good one," Mike said.

I laughed. "Me, too."

"So what are you going to do about Sue?" Mike asked.

"I'm planning to head over to her place in a bit. Try to talk to her face to face. Get this whole mess straightened out."

"Good luck, buddy. I hope it works out. I know Gina does, too."

"How's things going between you and Gina?"

"Good. We talked to Jack about moving into Gina's house, and he's good with that, as long as his room is as far away from the baby as he can get."

I laughed.

"He's had enough of listening to his baby sister cry in the middle of the night at his mom's. That was really his only request. Well, besides the request that the baby be a boy."

"Do you care if it's a boy or a girl?" I asked.

"Are you kidding me? Absolutely not. I just can't believe that Gina and I are actually having a child together. I mean, this is a dream come true. I'm still pinching myself just to make sure it's all real."

"I'm happy for you, man. You guys are proof that sometimes things do work out. It might take a while, but eventually it does."

"Go talk to Sue, Tom. And I hope things work out for you, too."

Sue

I noticed my yearbook on the desk in the kitchen. I guess I never put it away after the reunion. I grabbed it. I figured I'd look at it while I ate.

I was paging through it when I came to the Senior Man of the Year pages. The yearbook staff had chosen eight guys and the senior class voted on the nominees. The winner was announced at the Winter Sports Pep Rally. The nominees were Mike and Keith, Jeremy and Eric, Brad, J.R., Tom, and Frank. And Tom had won. I'd forgotten about this.

Tom looked so young. I guess we all did. Back then, who knew how our lives would unfold, where we'd end up. I could've guessed Tom would be a pharmacist, given his love of chemistry and science. And that Jeremy would follow in his dad's footsteps and become a dentist. But I'd never had imagined that Gina would end up being a prosecutor or that Karen, who got pregnant in high school, would end up falling in love with another woman and having her child. I guess that's the thing about life. Sometimes it takes you down unexpected roads.

I closed my yearbook and grabbed my keys.

Tom

I jumped in my car and realized I wasn't going to get too far unless I got gas. So, I stopped at the gas station next to the Interstate on-ramp. It was faster taking the highway and getting off at the Queen Street exit to get to Sue's than snaking through town.

I was heading south on the Interstate feeling life. I kept rehearsing what I was going to say to Sue. How I was going to handle the conversation. I needed to make her see how much I cared for her.

By the time I got there, I felt prepared. I felt good. But then I knocked on the door, and she didn't answer. I thought maybe she knew it was me and wasn't answering the door on purpose, so I peeked in her garage window to see if her car was there. No car. Shit! I guess she's not at home.

Sue

I kept ringing and ringing Tom's doorbell. His Ford was in the garage, but I noticed his '58 MG wasn't. Still, it could be in the garage. He'd said something about getting new tires on it. So I got out my cell phone and called.

He answered on the first ring. "Sue. Please. Don't hang up."

"Uh. I was the one who called you, so why would I hang up?"

"Guess you're right," he said. "Look, I want to talk."

"Me, too."

"Where are you?" he asked.

"At your house."

"That's funny because I'm at your house."

I told him to stay at my house, and I'd come to him.

"Are you sure?" he asked.

"Yes. I'll be right there. You can let yourself in. There's a key under the flower pot on the back porch."

I returned to my car and headed home.

Tom

I found the key right where Sue said it would be. I let myself in and noticed our high school yearbook was sitting on the kitchen table. It was open to the Senior Man of the Year pages. God, I'd forgotten about the contest and that I somehow managed to win.

I do remember the night, though, when the girls had to dress like boys and the guys had to dress like girls and we paraded around the homecoming bonfire. I paged through the yearbook looking for those pages and found them. I laughed out loud.

Mike wore one of his grandma's floral dresses. He'd stuffed a pillow in his gut and tons of tissues in a bra he borrowed from Gina. I could still hear our conversation in the locker room getting ready for the event.

"How do I look?" Mike had asked, parading around, throwing his hips from one side to the other.

"It's a good thing you're not a girl," Jeremy teased. "'Cause you make one ugly chick."

Everyone laughed at each other. I bought a dress and shoes at the Goodwill store to wear. I can still remember how much my feet hurt wearing those high heels. They mashed my toes together. I never could understand how a woman could wear those things. They seemed so uncomfortable.

I got lost looking at the yearbook and found myself smiling more than I'd smiled in a long time.

Chapter 12

Sue

I couldn't get to Tom fast enough. What were the chances that each of us would be at the other's house at the same time? Talk about bad timing.

I kept thinking about what I'd say to him. My cell phone rang. It was in my purse, which had fallen off the front seat and onto the floor. I could tell by the ring that it was Gina, probably checking up on me. I reached down to get my purse, having to stretch a little farther than I anticipated. I answered the phone and when I sat back up I realized I was over the yellow line. The driver in the oncoming car was blowing his horn. I swerved back over into my lane but skidded and found myself airborne.

There were sirens and flashing lights. I was pinned in my car, which was on its roof. My heart raced. I imagined the car was going to burst into flames at any moment. I thought of Chloe and how I wasn't going to see her grow up, marry, and have children of her own. My chest hurt. I was having trouble breathing. Blood was everywhere. I could taste it in my mouth. I could hear Gina yelling my name.

"Sue! Sue! Are you all right! Sue! Answer me!"

And then everything went black.

Tom

I kept checking the clock. Where was Sue? I'd expected her to be home by now. I called her cell, but it kept going into voicemail. Maybe she changed her mind about wanting to talk. But I wasn't going anywhere. I figured sooner or later she had to come home. I wasn't going to lose her again.

An hour passed and then another thirty minutes. Just when I was thinking that leaving might not be a bad idea after all, give Sue more time if she wasn't quite ready, there was a knock at the door. It was Mike and he looked white.

"Mike, what's up? You look terrible."

Mike stepped inside. "It's Sue. She's been in an accident."

"Oh God. Is she okay? Where is she?"

"At the hospital. That's all I know. Gina was on the phone with Sue when it happened. Gina heard everything. She's taking the first flight she can get home. I'll take you to the hospital."

"And Chloe?"

"Sue called her," Mike explained. "She was at the mall with her girlfriend. Her dad is going to pick her up and take her to the hospital."

I locked Sue's door and jumped into Mike's car. "Fuck! I can't lose her now, Mike. We were going to talk, work everything out."

"Gina told me," Mike said. "Think positive thoughts, Tom. We won't know how bad the accident was until we get to the hospital."

Mike and I pulled into the emergency room parking lot right behind Chloe and her dad.

I jumped out of the car and ran over to Chloe. "Hear anything?"

Her face was red and blotchy. She shook her head. "I only know what Aunt Gina said. She was talking to Mom when it happened."

We walked inside and were whisked back to a small room. Mike and Steve stayed in the waiting room.

When the nurse opened the door, Sue's mom was inside, sitting on a vinyl couch with a big box of tissues by her side.

"Gram," said Chloe, sitting down beside her. "Is Mom going to be all right? Did you hear anything yet?"

Chloe remembered I was in the room. "Grandma, you remember Tom, right?"

Grandma nodded. "Thank you for coming, Tim. I mean Tom. Can I just call you T? I have trouble remembering names."

"'T' is fine," I told her.

The doctor walked into the room. "Hi. I'm Dr. Andersen." He shook each of our hands. "I've been taking care of Sue." He looked at Chloe. "Are you Sue's daughter?"

Chloe nodded.

Sue's mother stood. "And I'm her mother. Is my Suzy going to be all right?"

"She has some serious injuries," Dr. Andersen said. "We had to reduce the swelling and pressure on the brain, which can cut off blood flow and kill healthy brain tissue. By reducing the brain activity, we lessen the pressure. Sue wasn't responding to other measures, so we had to place her in a drug-induced coma. Give the brain time to heal."

"Will she come out of it?" Chloe asked.

Dr. Andersen nodded. "We put the brain to sleep using sedatives. And we'll closely monitor the brain's activity. We'll keep it asleep for a couple of days. Just to get your mom through this critical period. Then we'll wean her off the drugs, bring her out of it."

"You mean wake her up?" Chloe asked.

"Yes, once the pressure starts to stabilize, we'll reduce the medicine and start the waking process. If the pressure starts to increase, we might have to slow it down," Dr. Andersen said.

The doctor said some more stuff about fractured ribs and a punctured lung, but it was all a blur. The only thing I could think about was Sue, how much I wanted to hold her and tell her I loved her. And my greatest fear was that I'd never get that chance.

～

I've never felt so helpless in all my life. The days seemed to crawl by. Each day after work, I'd visit Sue. Even though I wasn't immediate family, Chloe and her grandmother told them I was Sue's boyfriend, and they allowed me into the ICU.

I was getting daily updates from Gina, who was staying with Chloe. Gina had told me that she hated to leave, but she had to fly home. She had that co-ed rape case to prepare. She wanted to wrap up the case before moving back for good. I knew Gina had a lot to do and promised her I'd keep her updated, just like she had kept me updated.

I hated seeing Sue hooked up to all of the machines. I'd never seen so many gadgets and gizmos and wires.

I kept replaying my last conversation with Sue over in my mind, and I was mad that I hadn't insisted she be the one to stay put. If I would have, the accident never would've happened.

"No. It was my fault," Gina had said. "I called her. Probably distracted her."

"Sue didn't have to answer the phone," I told Gina. "She could've let it go into voicemail. You know the last thing she'd want is for you to blame yourself. And if we really want to blame someone, we should blame Rachel. If she hadn't been in my house waiting for me in that stripper get-up, none of this would've happened. Sue and I would've been together that night."

I knew that talking about what-ifs was useless. And blaming ourselves wasn't productive, either. But it was hard not to do.

I spent hours holding Sue's hand, telling her that she had to be strong, had to fight. That, damn it, we had a life to live together.

News of the accident spread quickly, and Sue's friends offered to do anything they could. They dropped off meals at the house, offered to run Chloe to dance lessons. Even her ex, Steve, was pretty decent. I still didn't like the guy, but at least he was taking good care of Chloe. Sue was right, he might be a jerk to her, but he adored his daughter.

～

Chloe and I were sitting by Sue's bed chatting when Dr. Andersen came by. He flipped open Sue's chart. "How's our girl doing?"

I sat up straight. "You tell us, Doc."

He flipped through the papers. "She's doing well. In fact, I think it's time to start the weaning process."

Chloe clapped her hands. "You're going to wake her up?"

Dr. Andersen nodded. "We'll slowly reduce the amount of anesthesia we're giving your mom. It's been a few days, and she's doing well. If there's no increase in brain pressure, we'll continue to decrease the drug. But if the pressure in the brain jumps, we'll have to increase it again. Do you have any questions?"

"Will she be all right when she wakes up?" Chloe asked.

"I hope so," Dr. Andersen said. "She might be a little confused. Maybe even a bit annoyed and irritated. Just have patience."

"When will you start?" I asked.

"Tonight."

When I returned home, I called Gina to tell her the good news. She was still at the office when I called.

"You're there awfully late," I said.

"Yeah. I'm determined to nail these bastards. I hope you have good news, because I could use some right now."

"Doctor Andersen said he's going to bring Sue out of the coma."

Gina's scream hurt my eardrum. "Sorry," she said. "I'm just so excited. "How long will it take to wake her up?"

"Depends. He said he'll turn down the anesthesia, and as long as the brain pressure doesn't increase, he'll continue to dial it down."

"What if the pressure increases?" Gina asked.

"Then he has to administer more of the drug. So let's hope he can back down the drug and Sue's brain pressure is stable."

"But he thinks she's going to be okay, right?" Gina asked.

"Yes. But he did say she might be confused."

"I'll be home next week," Gina said. "I wish I could come home earlier, but I just can't. Damn, I hate living so far away."

"Well, you won't be for long. How's the house coming along, anyway?"

"I just got off the phone with Mike, and he said I'd be pleased. The new roof's on, the house has been painted; it's all going according to plan. "

"Great. Glad to hear that."

I told Gina about my plan. "I figured when Sue comes home, she'll need someone to stay with her. I know her Mom said she would, but I kind of want to be the one to take care of her."

"Did you tell Sue's mom that?"

"Yes. And she said that as long as Sue was okay with it, she was, too. She said she would come over and stay with Sue during the day while I'm at work and Chloe is in school."

"Sounds like you have it all figured out," Gina said.

"Yeah, now we just need Sue to come out of the coma and be okay."

Chapter 13

Sue

I woke up to a mess of wires, bleeping machines, and tubes. And fear.

I heard a deep voice. "She opened her eyes."

I was confused. I didn't know where I was. Seemed like a bed. I yanked at the thing in my mouth. What was it? I couldn't breathe. People swarmed the bed. They were disconnecting tubes.

There were more voices. Questions. Commands.

A haze of people and sounds and movements.

"Where am I?" I mumbled. My throat felt dry.

"In the hospital," the deep voice said. I recognized the voice, but I couldn't remember. I hate that feeling of almost remembering but having it slip away. It's like swimming toward the beach and just when you're about to reach the shore the water pulls you back out. You're so close, but not quite there.

"Sue, it's me, Tom."

Tom. Familiar name. I was reaching for the shore. Reaching.

Reaching.

I felt a warm hand cup my hand. "Sue, I'm so glad to see you awake. Everything is going to be okay."

It seemed to take days before I reached the shore. When I finally made it, I recognized Tom and Chloe. I didn't remember anything that happened. Tom and Chloe fed me bits and pieces. I think they were afraid of overwhelming me. I learned I'd been in a drug-induced coma for several days following a terrible accident. But the last thing I remember was having shower sex with Tom, and it made me smile.

Tom

Watching Sue was like watching the little arrow on the computer screen going round and round, waiting for a website to load. Her consciousness was gradually improving. There were times when she opened her eyes and stared into space, but she wasn't quite awake, and they'd close again.

But finally the arrow stopped. Sue opened her eyes, this time pulling at the tubes and wires, and I knew she'd come back to me. She mumbled. She wanted to know where she was. I remembered what the doctor had said about not giving her too much information too fast. So I waited, answering her questions as they came up.

Still, I wanted to tell her that I loved her. I didn't want another hour to go by without her knowing.

But I knew I had to be patient. I didn't know if she had any memory loss. The doctor said she might not remember the events right before the accident. It was killing me not to know if Sue remembered the whole Rachel fiasco. I thought it would be great if she didn't. It would make things so much easier. But the rational part of my brain kicked in, and I realized that was the easy way out.

And if Sue didn't remember, I wouldn't feel right keeping that kind of thing from her. It would be akin to keeping a secret, one that everyone knew except Sue. And, most secrets have a way of coming out. Sue would really be furious with me then. Maybe I'd even lose her for good. No. I just had to be patient. See if the bits and pieces came to her, and when they did deal with them the best I could.

Gina was right. Sue's memory loss could've been worse. I don't know what I would've done if she wouldn't have remembered me and what we had become to each other in recent weeks.

Finally, after what seemed like years spent in the chair next to Sue's bed, the doctor said she could go home. I took off work, and Sue's mom, Rosa, and I decided we'd bring her home together. Chloe wanted to take off school, but Sue insisted Chloe go because she'd missed so much already.

◠ ◡

"You like my Suzy a lot, don't you, T?" asked Rosa on our way to the hospital.

I nodded. "I always have. Even in high school."

She put a mint in her mouth. "What took you so long, then?"

I stuttered. "She always had a boyfriend."

"No good ones," Rosa said. "You would've been a good one."

I smiled. "Thanks. Good to know you would've approved."

"Still do."

"What?"

"Approve. In fact, I think you should marry my Suzy."

I coughed. It was clear who Sue got her spunkiness from. And her height, pale eyes, and blonde hair. The woman was definitely put together. I noticed that her shoes always matched her outfit. And I imagined she had a closet full of flats in every possible color.

"I think it's a little too soon to talk about marriage, don't you?"

Rosa waved her hand. "Baloney, boy. If you want something, go get it. If you're too slow, the other boys will beat you every time."

I choked but couldn't hold back my laughter. "You should've given me that talk in high school."

"Well, I'm given it to you now. My Suzy needs a real man. Not one who thinks he is. I know Steve is Chloe's dad, but the creep thinks his one-eye snake is king of the jungle. I think it's a dried up worm. The only good thing that ever came out of that dick was Chloe."

I started laughing. "I'm sorry. I can't help it."

She winked. "There's something you need to understand about women, T. Sometimes we play hard to get when what we really want is to be caught and held. The trick is letting us think we've outsmarted you. Do you think you can do that?"

"What?"

"Let Sue think she's outsmarted you."

"I can try, if you think that'll work."

"If we're lucky, she's ready to be caught. Good Lord, I hope so. I want to see her married before I'm dead."

"You're not ill, are you?"

Rosa shook her tiny head. "Hell, no. But you never know when the good Lord will call me home. And when

I get called to go home, I want to make sure my Suzy has a man worthy of her. And from the way you've been at her bedside every day, I'd say you'd be a pretty good candidate. Do you make much money?"

I coughed again.

"You don't have to answer that," Rosa said. "But I don't want my Suzy to settle for someone who can't afford to take her out to dinner or on a nice vacation."

"I don't think you have to worry about that with me," I told her.

Rosa nodded. "Good."

I was relieved when I pulled into the hospital parking lot. I'd never spent so much time alone with Rosa, and I was just beginning to realize what a firecracker the woman was. I could see where Sue got her no-bullshit ways.

Sue

I was thinking about a nightmare I had the night before when the discharge nurse came into my room.

"Ready to go home?" she asked, placing the clean clothes Chloe had brought in the night before on my bed.

I nodded.

"You look like you were in deep thought," she said. "Everything okay?"

"I was just remembering this horrible nightmare."

"Want to share it? Maybe it'll make you feel better."

I shrugged my shoulders. "I was stuck in a dryer, and it was going round and round and round. I couldn't open the door from the inside to get out, and everyone kept coming to the dryer and looking in, watching me spin round and round but not opening the door to help me. It was horrible. It was dark and hot, and I became dizzy and no one would help me."

I started to cry, and that's when Mom and Tom walked into the room.

Mom rushed to my bedside and hugged me. "What's wrong with my Suzy?"

I sniffed. "I'll be all right, Mom. Just remembering a bad dream, that's all."

"Do you need us to get you anything?" Tom asked.

I shook my head. "I just want to get out of here and go home."

A wheelchair ride later from the sixth floor to the discharge ramp on the first floor and I was headed home. Mom was riding shotgun, and I was in the back.

"Gina should be over tonight," Tom said. "Mike is picking her up at the airport at 5, and I know she wants to see you first thing."

"How's her house coming?" I asked.

"Mike said it's going great. Thinks Gina will be pleased. He said Jack loves his new room."

I laughed. "Jack's a sweet kid."

"Yeah, Mike said we'll have to go out for dinner when Gina gets back in town."

"Didn't we just recently go out to dinner with them?"

Sue surprised me. I knew from talking to her what her last memory was. The dinner happened after that.

"Do you remember that?" I asked.

"Not completely," Sue said. "A little. Mostly the champagne."

A sigh of relief escaped my lips. I had a lump in my throat, nervous that she'd remember Rachel and what happened several days later. It didn't come—yet. But I knew it was only a matter of time.

"Don't worry," Rosa said. "You'll remember. And when you get to be my age, you'll be glad if there are things you did that you could forget. Like the time I left a tampon in my chocha?"

"Mom! Please! I'm sure Tom doesn't want to hear about your chocha."

I had a view of Tom from the back seat and I could see he was mashing his lips together, trying not to laugh.

"Well, at least I didn't get an 8-ball stuck up there."

"Mom! I mean it! You're embarrassing me."

Tom couldn't hold it back any longer. He laughed. "Do you mean an 8-ball as in a billiard ball?"

"That's exactly what I mean," Mom said. "Heard it at the hairdresser's. Janice told Karen and Karen told me, but I wasn't supposed to tell anyone, so don't repeat it. Turned out the girl had to go to her ob-gyn to get the darn thing removed. Now that's something you'd want to forget."

I was so happy when we pulled up to my house.

Tom

Rosa was definitely a character. I liked her. She made me laugh, even though I knew Sue wanted to crawl under the back seat.

I helped Sue into the house.

"I think I'd like to lay down for a bit," Sue said. "I'm feeling kind of tired."

"Where do you want to rest?" Rosa asked.

"In my bed. I feel as if I haven't slept well in forever."

"T, why don't you take Suzy upstairs, and I'll make this casserole for later."

I looked at Sue. "I could just carry you up. That might be easiest."

Sue smiled, and I scooped her up and carried her upstairs. When I put her down on her bed, she pulled me toward her.

"Thank you for everything," she said.

I looked into her pale blue eyes. I didn't know if I should, but I wanted to kiss her. God how I wanted to kiss her, to let her know that I was never going to leave her side, unless she wanted me to.

Our lips found one another and we kissed long and hard.

"You know what I'm thinking about?" Sue whispered.

"What?"

She smiled. "The shower sex."

I nodded. "That's a good memory, right?"

"Very good," Sue said. "Want to rest beside me?"

"But your mom's downstairs."

"I'm nearly 40," Sue said. "And besides, it's not like we're going to make love. We're just going to rest. And it would be nice having you beside me."

I slipped into bed next to Sue and put my arm around her. It didn't take her long to fall asleep. She looked so peaceful, curled like a cat. I stared at her, drinking in every detail—long, feathery eyelashes; a tiny mole on her right temple; pink lips that looked more like a child's than those of a mature woman. She was beautiful. So different from Rachel in every way imaginable.

I hated that Rachel entered my thoughts while I lay beside Sue. I wondered if Sue would remember finding Rachel in my house and, if she did, if she'd be angry all over again and push me away. I couldn't stand it if that happened again. Once was bad enough. I feel horrible saying this, but I dreaded the day her memory fully returned.

Chapter 14

Sue

I slept for a couple of hours, and when I woke up, I felt Tom's arm around my waist. He'd fallen asleep, too.

He woke up when I slipped out of bed to go to the bathroom. "I can't believe I fell asleep. I must've been more tired than I thought."

By the time we walked downstairs, Mom's casserole was cooling on top of the stove.

Mom looked up from reading the newspaper. "About time you two woke up. Casserole's ready if you're hungry."

"It smells delicious," Tom said.

I rubbed my stomach. "I'm hungry."

We decided to eat, and Tom set the table while Mom fixed a salad to go along with her chicken and broccoli dish.

"Do you remember the first time I made this dish?" Mom asked.

I smiled.

"Sounds like there's a story to be told," Tom said.

Mom jabbed a piece of broccoli. "Suzy always thought these looked like small trees, and she didn't like them. So I made this casserole, thinking that maybe she'd like them this way. And I thought she did when she cleaned her plate."

"But?" Tom asked.

Rosa nodded toward Sue. "Go ahead. Tell him."

I was embarrassed. "I sort of sneaked them into a napkin I had on my lap. Every time I stabbed a piece, instead of putting it in my mouth, I dropped it into the opened napkin. It worked great. Afterward, I threw the bundle of broccoli out."

"But," Rosa held up her finger. "What Suzy didn't count on was the dog getting into the trash and me finding the broccoli spilling from the napkin on the floor."

Tom laughed. "So what happened next?"

"I made it the next night for warm-ups," Mom said.

"And?" Tom asked.

I shrugged my shoulders. "I liked it."

Tom laughed.

"I told my Suzy that if you never give something a chance, how are you going to know if you like it? From then on, she was willing to take chances."

"And today I love it," Sue said.

Tom

I loved the broccoli story. And I kept thinking about Sue taking chances. She was willing to take a chance with me and Rachel screwed that up. Sooner or later, the memory of that night would return. All I could do is hope that when it did, Sue would give us another chance.

We were finishing dinner when Chloe bounced in the door. She ran and hugged Sue. "I'm so glad you're home."

"Grab a plate and join us," Rosa said.

Chloe sniffed. "What is it?"

"Chicken and broccoli," Rosa said.

Chloe scrunched her nose. "I hate broccoli."

We laughed.

"What's so funny?"

"I was just telling T about your mom hating broccoli and how when she actually tried it, she liked it."

"I'll eat it raw dipped in dressing, but never cooked," Chloe said. "Besides, I'm not real hungry. I'll get something later."

"Do you have a lot of homework?" Sue asked.

"Some."

"Why don't you get it done so you can visit when Aunt Gina gets here?"

Chloe grabbed her backpack and headed to her room, and I helped Sue to the living room so she could watch TV and relax while Rosa and I cleaned up.

I handed Rosa dinner plates to load in the dishwasher. "The casserole was delicious. Thanks for making it."

Rosa smiled. "I love cooking. Ever since Howe passed away, I don't do much of it anymore. Not fun cooking for yourself. That's why I enjoy when the family comes over for Sunday dinner. Do you cook much?"

I shook my head. "It's just me and Klondike, speaking of which, I need to get home to check on him. I had a neighbor take him out, but he's probably wondering where I am."

"We used to have a dog," Rosa said. "That old mutt was more kid than dog."

I smiled. "Sounds like Klondike."

Sue

"I'll be fine," I told Mom and Tom. "Chloe's upstairs, and Gina just called and said she'll be here in ten minutes."

"Well, if you're sure you're gonna be okay," Mom said. "I'll be back tomorrow morning before Chloe goes to school."

Mom went to get her things, and Tom sat beside me. "Do you want me to come back? I can bring Klondike with me and spend the night."

I smiled. "Sleeping beside you did feel great, but I hate for you to run home and then back again. Besides, Gina's coming, and you know how we are when we start talking."

Tom nodded. "Yeah, I definitely know what that's like."

I kissed Tom and Mom goodbye and dozed off. *I was in the dryer, spinning around and around and around. Tom looked in the window. And then Gina and Chloe and Mom looked in the window. I was banging on the dryer window, crying for help, but no one was helping me. They just took turns peeking in the window, watching me go around and around.*

"Help me! Help me!" I screamed. I woke up to hands shaking me.

"Sue, it's just a bad dream. Everything's okay. You're at home with me and Chloe."

I opened my eyes to find Chloe and Gina sitting next to me.

I was confused. "Where am I?"

"You're at home with me and Chloe," Gina repeated.

"Why didn't you help me get out of the dryer?" I cried.

Chloe bit her bottom lip. "Mom, you're scaring me."

"It was a bad dream, Sue," Gina said. "Just a bad dream. You're safe at home. Chloe and I are here. Everything's going to be okay."

I looked at Chloe, and her eyes were glassy.

"Are you all right, Mom? Aunt Gina and I were eating when you started to scream."

I reached out and took her hand. "I'm okay, Chloe. Just tired."

I wanted to tell Gina about the dream, but I didn't want Chloe to hear. No need to upset her.

"I brought your favorite ice cream," Gina said. "Want some?"

I smiled. Gina always knew how to make me smile.

We ate ice cream, and then Chloe went to finish studying and take her shower.

"So now that we're alone, how are things, really?" asked Gina, putting a throw pillow on her lap.

A heavy sigh escaped my lips. "Okay. I'm tired and still in some pain. It bugs me that I don't remember the accident. Or the day or so leading up to it. In fact, the last memory I have of Tom is having great shower sex."

Gina laughed. "Well, that's a good last memory to have."

"Don't get me wrong, I'm not complaining. But I can't help feeling like I'm missing something. It's hard to explain. Pretend my life is a tape and someone hit the pause button, abruptly stopping it. My life resumed later when the play button was pushed, but a section of tape became tangled when it was abruptly stopped. That tangled section is the missing memories. I've been trying to untangle the tape but it's stuck, and I can't seem to get it out in one piece."

"Maybe that's the problem," Gina said. "You're trying too hard. If I were you, I'd relax and enjoy life. Don't push yourself too hard to remember. Most likely, your memories will return when you aren't expecting them to."

I nodded. "Yeah, that's kind of what the doctor said. Something might trigger a memory. And there's a chance that I won't remember everything. But I'm getting glimpses of things. Like the dinner we had."

"The one at the fancy restaurant?"

I nodded. "That was the night before the shower sex morning. You had bought two bottles of champagne, and I drank a little too much."

"Does Tom know you remember that?" Gina asked.

"Yeah. I told him the last thing I remember was the shower sex. That made him smile."

"I bet it did," Gina said. "That's all you remember about that night?"

"Pretty much. Should I have remembered more?"

Gina shook her head. "You remembered enough."

Tom

When I opened the back door, Klondike was right inside waiting for me. While we were on a walk, Gina texted me, letting me know she was with Sue and that Sue was sleeping. I was glad Gina was able to spend some time with Sue. Gina and I had talked about Sue's memory loss. She was as concerned as I was about how Sue would handle the memory of seeing Rachel in my house dressed in her whore regalia. The doctor said it's not uncommon for a patient to not remember what happened right before the accident and that the memories could return in bits and pieces. We just had to be prepared to handle that when they did. Maybe I should've told the doctor about Rachel, since they weren't all good memories Sue lost.

Klondike wouldn't leave my side the rest of the night. We were watching TV when Sue called.

"I miss you," Sue said.

"I miss you, too. Feeling any better?"

"Still feel tired and weak."

"Well, remember what the doctor said. It might take a while."

Sue sighed. "I was wondering about your offer."

"You mean about me and Klondike staying over?"

"Yeah. I talked to Chloe, and she's fine with it. Actually more than fine. Well, not fine that you're coming over. That sounds terrible. Not that she minds you coming over, but she's more excited about having Klondike here."

I smiled. "Of course."

"Anyway, what do you think?"

"Nothing could keep me away," I said.

The three words I wanted to say were on the tip of my tongue, ready to slip off. But I held them back. I wanted Sue to be ready to hear them. Really hear them and know that I meant them.

Chapter 15

Sue

Gina invited some of our high school friends over to her house for a girls' night. No guys allowed. She thought it would be fun to reminisce and a great way to celebrate my recovery. She was able to pick a weekend when those who lived out of town could come.

I was looking forward to seeing the old gang—Diane, Lynn, Ellen, and Maggie. Karen was bringing her partner, Mia. And of course, Cookie, who always made me laugh so hard my gut hurt.

It took Cookie about two sips of wine before she fired her hairy ball question.

"So I was reading this magazine article about whether guys should shave their balls. What do you girls think? I, for one, am not a fan of ball hair."

The room erupted into laughter.

"I don't like caveman hairy," Diane said. "A trim is good, but definitely not bald. That makes me think of a little boy and totally grosses me out."

Lynn took a sip of wine. "Personally, I think guys' balls are effing ugly. They look like one of those rubber chickens."

"Especially if the balls are bare and the dick is limp," Maggie added.

I laughed so hard I had to hold my gut. The laughing was good for my mind, but not my healing ribs.

"I agree with Diane," Gina said. "Some hair is okay. But not so long that you can braid it. I never let mine get that long!"

"Me neither," Karen says, looking at Mia. "We like bare best."

Cookie laughed so hard she fell off the barstool.

"You know," Mia said. "Some men shave their pubes because it makes their dicks look bigger."

Karen narrowed her eyes and looked at her partner. "How would you know?"

Uh oh! I thought maybe we were going to have a girl fight in Gina's kitchen.

"Like you, love," said Mia, her lips curling into a sexy smile. "I've had a man or two in my life. Just decided I liked the other team better."

I'm not sure if Cookie thought she needed to diffuse the tension, but she blurted, "And another thing, I think guys should dip their dicks in Scope. They'd taste so much better!"

"Try putting whipped cream on it," Ellen said. "And maybe a little chocolate syrup."

We all howled.

"Well, you are the chef," Cookie laughed. "It makes sense that you'd be able to tell us how to doctor up a dog to make it more palatable."

There was more laughter.

Gina, who was the only one who wasn't drinking, said, "Man, I wish I could have what you're all having."

"How's the mommy-to-be, anyway?" Karen asked. "You look great."

Gina rubbed her hand over her stomach. "I feel great. I'm not puking as much as I was, so that's good. I'm still tired, but even that seems to be getting a little better. What surprises me most are my boobs. Damn! I never thought I'd have boobs this big."

"You want to talk about boobs, girlfriend," said Cookie, holding hers, one in each hand. "These girls got so big I thought I might have to wear a sling around my neck to keep them from dragging on the ground. We're talking serious tonnage."

There was more laughter.

"So are you going to find out what you're having?" Mia asked.

"I want to know; Mike doesn't. So, we haven't decided what we'll do yet."

"I wanted to know," Lynn said. "I wanted to make sure the room was tailored to the sex."

I wasn't surprised by Lynn's admission. She was, after all, an events planner. She was the type of person who wanted everything coordinated and paid attention to the tiniest of details. She'd already cornered me about having a surprise baby shower for Gina.

The night was just what I needed. I even had a little wine. It was great to be with friends who you could unwind with and be yourself. And talk about things like hairy balls and dick sundaes.

Tom

Gina had invited the girls to her house so I decided I'd invite the guys over to my house. Grill some burgers, drink some beer. Maybe play some poker. Good times.

Jeremy had a fight with Teresa right before he arrived and the first twenty minutes was spent listening to him rant about it.

"So she's on me about not fixing the faucet. Tells me I don't do my share when it comes to hauling the kids around. Then she's on me about never saying anything nice to her. Which, by the way, is pure bullshit. Christ, I couldn't wait to get out of there. Talk about PMS."

"You do know why they call it PMS, don't you?" asked Keith, not waiting for an answer. "Because Mad Cow was taken."

Everyone laughed.

"Besides, guys never say all that sweet shit they say in the movies," said Keith, screwing off the cap on his bottle of beer. "And why do we have to work so damn hard to get sex? I'd like a massage every once in a while, too!"

I laughed.

"You just wait, lover boy," Jeremy said. "When you've been with someone as long as we have, the sex sort of loses its steam."

I was glad when the conversation turned to sports and cars, the normal topics guys talk about.

"You still have your 58?" Keith asked.

I nodded.

Jeremy sipped his beer. "Man, I'd love to restore an old car. With two college educations to pay for, that's not going to happen."

Jeremy patted Mike on the shoulder. "Mikey here is catching up to me, though. In a few months you'll have two."

Mike nodded. "Yep. Can't wait."

"Man, there's no way I'd want to go back to having a screaming kid in the middle of the night. That's a pain in the ass," Jeremy said.

There was more talk and more beer, and a few hours later, we had solved all of the world's problems. Life was good.

Sue

"Who likes to screw in the morning?" Ellen asked.

"Not me," said Diane, shaking her head. "I don't know any woman who likes sex first thing in the morning."

"I do," said Lynn, sitting up straight and bouncing side to side. "Kind of gets me going. Like eating a big bowl of Wheaties. Gives me lots of energy."

Mia laughed. "The breakfast of champions."

"I'm with Diane on this one," Maggie said. "Most women I know give in and bury their face in the pillow so they don't have to smell their breath."

"Do what I do,' Cookie said. "Keep a tiny bottle of mint mouth spray under your pillow. Pull it out and give him a squirt and then yourself."

Lynn laughed. "I'm impressed with your planning skills, Cookie. I didn't know you had that in you."

Cookie smiled. "You might be the events planner in the group, Lynn, but I'm the survivor of the sex wilderness. This Girl Scout knows how to prepare."

Growing up, whenever we got together, we always played Question/Answer. It was sort of like a game. Someone would throw out a question, and we'd all answer it. When we got older, we held on to the tradition. Only the questions we ask now are a bit X-rated.

"What's the most embarrassing thing that ever happened to you?" I asked.

Gina laughed. "You know what mine was. It was the Boeing 747 fart I let rip during my violin recital."

Everyone laughed.

"I remember I was on a wooden stage, and I tapped my shoe extra loud to try to drown it out. I could feel my face heat up. I'm sure it was the color of a candy apple."

"What about you, Diane?"

"Well, here's something that happened today. I'm at the stop light and I look down and realize that the damn bra pads in my dress are scrunched up. Unlike my bathing suit, there were no holes in the dress where I could stick my finger in and smooth the pads out. So I'm at the stop light, both hands on my boobs, trying to smooth out the damn pads. And I'm really going at it, having a hell of a time. All of a sudden, I look over and realize that the guy in the car next to me has been watching me the whole time."

We all laughed.

"So what'd you do?" I asked.

"I tried to explain to him using sign language that I wasn't playing with my tits like he thought I was, but trying to smooth out the pads. Thank God the light turned green. When I got home, I threw out the dress."

The room erupted in laughter again.

"Who's next?" Gina asked.

"I'll go," Maggie said. "So I'm naked, and I have on these killer heels. James likes when I wear my whore heels in bed."

"What is it about fuck me heels on a naked girl that turns guys' dicks into homing missiles?" Cookie asked.

Everyone laughed.

"Anyway," Maggie continued. "We're in bed, and before I know it, my whore heels scratch his scrotum."

"Ouch," everyone said at the same time.

"Yeah," Maggie nodded. "It wasn't pretty. Totally killed the mercy screw I was giving him because he had to have a colonoscopy the next day."

"No shit," said Cookie, shaking her head.

"Actually," Maggie said, "by then he didn't have any shit left in him."

I laughed so hard my jaw hurt. I think it's true what they say about laughter being the best medicine. I know I was feeling much better than I had in a long time.

Tom

By the end of the night, we went through some serious suds and some not so serious talk.

"You did it every day for thirty-one days?" Jeremy asked after listening to Keith brag about his recent feat.

Keith grabbed a handful of Doritos. "Yeah, Kris read it in one of her magazines. She wanted to try it. At first, I thought it would be a little too much."

"Too much? What are you? A fucking idiot?" Jeremy laughed. "Do you think Kris would talk to Teresa, maybe suggest this 31-day deal? She's always trying new diet plans. Hell, maybe she'd try this."

Keith laughed. "Are you kidding me? She'd kill me if she knew I said anything. You just got to get creative, Jer. Try new things."

Jeremy looked at all of us. "Am I the only one not getting fucked on a regular basis?"

"I thought Teresa had a pole in your bedroom," Mike said.

"Yeah, for exercising."

We laughed.

"Okay. I'm all ears. What works?" asked Jeremy, straightening up on the bar stool.

Normally, guys don't get into details about sex, but this wasn't a normal group of guys. We shared a history. We'd witnessed each other's first kiss when we played spin the bottle in Becky's garage in sixth grade. We always had each other's back, whether it was bumming a condom on a night we didn't expect to score or throwing a couple of bucks in the pot for gas to get to the mall and back.

Keith crunched his Doritos. "Kris did this thing where she put a dab of chocolate syrup five different places on her body, and I had to find it. She blindfolded me, plus it was dark, so I couldn't see."

"Jesus fuckin' Christ, Keith," Jeremy said. "Now I really need Kris to talk to Teresa."

"Did you find all five?" Mike asked.

Keith nodded. "And then I did it."

"Go Keith! Go Keith! Go Keith!" we all chanted.

Keith shook his finger. "I swear, you better not say anything to Kris. Then I'll be the one who never gets it."

"So Mikey," Keith said. "You and Gina going to get married?"

"Absolutely. We can't wait. It's all we've ever wanted. I'm still pinching myself that it's really going to happen. We both want to get married as soon as possible, but we haven't nailed down a date yet. Don't worry, you'll all be invited."

Jeremy looked at me. "What about you, Tom? You think you and Sue will end up together?"

"I hope so. I really hope so."

Chapter 16

Sue

Gina's living room was a sea of sleeping bags. We moved the furniture to the sides and crammed into the space just like we did when we were kids. We even ended the night with a pillow fight. I'd forgotten how much fun they were. When we woke up the next morning, we looked like we were extras for *The Walking Dead*. Except Gina.

Maggie yawned and pointed at Gina. "You have no right to look that good."

Cookie laughed. "That reminds me of the time I thought I was pregnant and wasn't."

"Was this before or after the girls?" I asked.

"After. In fact, it was last year."

I coughed. "What? But I thought Harry had a vasectomy?"

"He did. About ten years ago!"

Everyone stopped getting breakfast to listen to Cookie's story.

"So, I'm gaining weight, you know," said Cookie, talking with her hands. "And I'm thinking my tits feel tender. And I can't remember when I had my period last. Since Harry had a vasectomy, I don't keep track of it, and my periods never were real regular anyhow. And I know people who have gotten pregnant after the old snip-snip."

"Yeah, like within a year," Lynn laughed. "Not a decade."

"Well, you never know," Cookie continued. "Could be that old snake had some venom left in him. God knows it doesn't seem to have a whole hell of a lot of life left in it these days, but, well, if I can get the damn thing up it does okay."

Everyone laughed.

"Anyway," Cookie continued. "The more I thought about the possibility of being pregnant, the more convinced I became that I actually was. So I buy not one home pregnancy test but two. You know, just to make sure. And I sneak into the bathroom when everyone else is downstairs and do the test. Not once, but twice. And..."

Cookie pauses and looks at each of us. "Turns out I was just getting fat. Damn pregnancy test. Those things suck!"

"You didn't want to be pregnant, did you?" Gina asked.

"Not really," Cookie said. "But it would've been nice to have been able to blame my belly fat on something other than cakes and cookies."

Everyone laughed so hard we looked like we were having a group seizure.

Cookie pinched her belly fat. "I could be a model for those belly fat ads online. Christ, every time I turn around another one pops up on my computer screen. I swear those ads have eyeballs, and when they see someone fat sit down in front of the screen they pop up. They're evil."

Cookie was a character—always was and always would be.

Tom

I filled a huge cardboard box with empty beer bottles. We definitely went through the brew. It was already mid-morning, and most of the guys had gone home, taking their hangovers with them. Mike stayed to help clean up. The kitchen looked like it had been hit by a hurricane. Guys could be real slobs.

Mike tossed the empty pizza boxes and chip and pretzel bags into a large trash bag. "I had a great time. Thanks for having us all over. It was a lot of fun."

I nodded. "Yeah, it was. We'll have to do it again. Felt like it did when we were in high school."

Mike laughed. "The joking and messing around did; my body did not. Definitely can't drink like I used to."

"Mike," I said. "You know Sue pretty well, right?"

"I guess so. I mean, I knew her better in high school, but yeah, I guess I know her better than most of the guys who were here. Why? What's up?"

"I'm worried that if her memory of finding Rachel in my house returns, she'll be pissed off again. I don't want to lose her."

"But if she remembers that, won't she also remember she was on her way to talk it out with you, to make up?"

I shrugged. "That's what I hope will happen. That's what I want to happen. But who knows."

Mike shook his head. "I know you're in a tough place. I think you're just going to have to ride this out. See what happens and hope for the best."

I poured myself another cup of coffee. "What about you and Gina? How's that going?"

Mike got another cup, too, and sat down at the table. "Absolutely fantastic. I can't wait to call her my wife. It's all I've ever wanted."

I sipped my coffee. "And it took damn near twenty years."

"About that," Mike said.

Sooner or later I knew Mike would want to talk. I knew he'd have questions about the night Gina was raped, the night I punched Coach Smith in the face when I learned what he'd done. And I knew that he would go off on me for not telling.

Mike ran his fingers through his hair. "I don't blame you. I don't. But damn, I wish you would've said something back then."

"I wish I would've, too. You don't know how many hours I've spent beating myself up over the decision I made that day. I thought Gina should be the one to tell. I still think it should've come from her, but I wish I would've confronted her about it, told her that I knew. Maybe then she wouldn't have felt so all alone. Maybe then she would've gone to the police, knowing she had me as a witness. Not to the rape, of course. But to Smith's confession afterward."

Mike let out a heavy sigh. "I just wonder how my life, our life, would've turned out. Maybe we would've stayed together."

"And maybe not," I said. "Sometimes, I think that you and Gina splitting up was for the best. She had a lot of demons to deal with. I'm not sure she could've dealt with them like she needed to and worry about you at the same time. So she did what she had to do. And she got well, and she became a killer prosecutor who puts bastards like Smith in jail. I know it's not the life you would've wanted for her, but she's helped a lot of people and, besides, you're together now."

Mike smiled. "Yeah. Crazy how it all happened so fast and yet it seems so right."

"I think that's called love, man."

"I think you're right."

Sue

"What's all the laughing about?" said Mia, walking into the kitchen dressed like she was headed down the runway at a New York fashion show. She wore a black sleeveless split-neck jacquard dress with a pleated skirt. The woman was drop-dead gorgeous.

Cookie whistled. "Man, oh man, Karen. If I were gay, I'd be fighting you for some of that skin."

"Well, then it's a good thing you're not," said Karen, kissing Mia on the cheek.

Everyone laughed.

Mia had showered and dressed because she had to leave to show an out of town client some properties.

"And look at those heels," Cookie said. "They must be eight inches. I sprain my ankle just looking at those suckers."

I looked at the strappy heels. They looked familiar. I had seen them before. I put my hand to my head and a memory flashed before my eyes.

"You all right, Sue?" asked Gina, grabbing my arm to steady me.

I shook my head. "It's a memory. A flash. Those heels. I've seen them before."

Mia held out her leg so everyone could see the black strappy heels that had triggered my memory.

"Do you want to sit down?" Gina asked.

"Yeah. That might be good."

Gina walked with me into the living room, navigating us through a sea of goodbyes and hugs.

"You guys don't have to leave," I said.

But no one listened. I think they wanted to give me some space and give me time alone with Gina. I was actually grateful, because I became a wet rag of tears that felt as heavy as cement blocks.

Tom

I was glad Mike and I talked about the rape. It was unfinished business. It was important to me that he understood why I didn't do anything twenty years ago. Doesn't make it right, but at least he knows where I was coming from. I think he needed to clear the air, say some things that were on his mind. I got that, and I wasn't mad. But I was glad he was moving on, trying to put it behind him.

I wasn't lying when I told Mike that I thought it was better he and Gina didn't stay together. I don't think it would've worked. There was too much trauma that Gina had to work through, and she needed to do that alone.

But I had to smile. Who would've thought twenty years later that they'd be back together—and be having a baby! And who would've thought I'd be dating the girl I've had a crush on since junior high earth science class.

I grabbed Klondike's leash. "Come on, boy. Let's go for that walk."

It was a beautiful Saturday, and the park was full of people. There were a lot of Little League baseball games going on. Seeing those little kids in their baseball shirts and hats always made me smile. Reminded me of when I was a kid. I loved baseball. Was never any good at it, but that didn't stop me from trying.

I figured by the time Klondike and I got back from our walk, Sue would be home from Gina's. She was expecting me and Klondike around 3. I told her I'd make my killer lasagna for her and Chloe and then maybe we'd go for a drive afterward.

She was getting stronger, and I knew by the way she kissed me that she wanted more. I was the one holding back. I just didn't feel right making love to her knowing our relationship had been strained prior to the accident. I kept thinking that when she remembered the Rachel fiasco, she might think I'd taken advantage of her memory loss by having sex with her while knowing that we were no longer at the having sex stage.

Chapter 17

Sue

I sat down on the couch and sobbed so hard my chest hurt. Finally, the dryer door was opened, and I was free, gasping for air, clawing to make sense of what I'd remembered.

Gina brushed back my hair. "So, did you remember, Sues?"

I nodded. "Rachel. She was at Tom's house when I took Klondike home. He was coming home from a conference, and I had this great evening planned. Even bought some sexy lingerie. But when I got there, I found Rachel, wearing a lacy thong and heart-shaped nipple covers with tassels."

I sniffed, and Gina handed me some more tissues.

"And I couldn't believe it was happening to me all over again. It was worse than when I found Steve screwing Little Miss Pierced Nipples. By the time he and Pierced Nipples had their mid-day fuck, I'd already suspected the creep was cheating. But Tom, no way would I ever have imagined Tom would do such a thing. I was crushed and left."

Gina bit her lower lip. "Do you remember what happened after that?"

"A little. I know I was pissed at Tom because Rachel had the key. But I don't remember the accident or being in the coma."

"Yes," Gina said. "You were pissed at Tom because he hadn't taken his key back from Rachel. But you were getting beyond it, and in fact, you were on your way to see him when the accident happened."

"I was?"

"Yes. You had gone to Tom's house to talk things out. He had gone to your house. When you both realized you were at each other's houses, you told Tom to wait at yours, and you would be right over. But you never got there—obviously."

"So we never did get to talk things out?" I asked.

"No," Gina said. "But Tom is the best thing that's ever happened to you, Sues. Don't let that man walk out of your life. He was by your side every day. He talked to you. Read to you for hours. Ask Chloe. She'll tell you. The man is head over heels in love with you, and I think if you're honest, you'll admit that you love him, too."

Tom

I was shopping in the pasta aisle, trying to decide between two brands of lasagna noodles when I heard Cookie's booming voice coming from the next aisle.

"Why does it have to be Heinz? Ketchup is ketchup. It's all alike. Just like men. You all drive me nuts."

I turned the corner to find Cookie staring at the rows of ketchup, talking on her cell phone.

"Okay. I'll buy the damn Heinz." She grabbed the bottle off the shelf and saw me when she turned.

"Hey, Tom. Have a good time last night with the guys?"

I smiled. It was great. "How'd the girls make out?"

"Had a blast. I don't think I've laughed so hard since high school. Have you talked to Sue yet today?"

I shook my head. "No, why?"

"Just wondered."

"Oh, no, Cookie. I can tell by the way your eye twitched you asked for a reason. Did something happen last night?"

"Not last night; this morning. But I don't want to be the one to say anything. I think you should talk to Sue or Gina. When I left, they were sitting on the sofa talking."

"Can you tell me anything?"

"I'm really not sure what happened. Mia, you know, Karen's partner, came down the stairs dressed for work. She was meeting a client from out of town. Anyway, she had on these strappy spike heels, and Sue said something about them looking familiar. After that, it got a little chaotic. I'm pretty sure Mia's whore heels must have triggered some sort of memory in Sue."

"Ah, fuck."

"Yeah, you probably would've wanted to fuck Mia. I told Karen that if I were gay I'd be giving her some stiff competition. That Mia is built, baby."

"No, I didn't mean that."

Cookie looked puzzled.

"How long ago was this?" I asked.

"Not that long ago. I stopped to get gas and came here after I left there, so maybe a half hour. Why?"

"I have to go. I'm supposed to make dinner for Sue tonight, and I need to make sure it's still on."

Sue

I hugged one of the throw pillows in Gina's couch. "I guess Tom and I have some talking to do, huh?"

Gina nodded. "Tom was furious when he learned what Rachel had done, Sues. By the following morning, he had changed all of the locks."

"It's just that it took me so long to allow myself to love again, you know? And when I finally decide to open my heart so honestly and completely it gets squashed."

"But Tom wasn't the one who squashed it," Gina said. "Rachel was. And Rachel only succeeds if you allow her to succeed. Don't. Don't walk away from this guy who's adored you forever, who loves you and wants to spend the rest of his life with you."

I sniffed. "Did he say that?"

"He didn't have to, Sues. We all can see it. The way his face brightens when you walk into a room. The way his eyes follow you. The guy has it bad."

"I think I have it bad, too."

Gina smiled. "Then tell him. Tell him how you feel."

I looked down at the couch.

"Look at me," Gina said. "I never thought I'd get a second chance with Mike. And here we are, going to get married and have a baby. Yes, I'm giving up a lot. I'm taking a chance. But I'd rather take the chance than spend any more of my life wondering what might have been.

"I think you're ready to take a chance, too. It just had to be the right person and the right time in your life. Chloe's getting older. She doesn't need you as much as she once did. You spent your whole life taking care of her. Now you need to take care of yourself. You might not get another chance."

I knew Gina was right. But I was still scared. Scared of where loving and taking chances would lead me. At the same time, I knew where I was headed if I didn't, and it was a lonely place to be.

Tom

Damn! There never seems to be enough check-out lines at the grocery store. Even the express wasn't express. I jumped in the shortest line, behind a woman in spandex that had no business being in spandex, holding a wad of coupons that would make any serious coupon clipper salivate.

The worst part? She was uber organized. Normally, I'd be amused watching someone group items together—cold with cold, boxes with boxes, cans with cans. But Spandex Mama took it a step further and had to make sure all of the barcodes were facing the cashier. No shit! While this lady was a wet dream for cashiers, she was pissing me off. The shortest line ended up being the longest line and by the time I left the store, I couldn't get to Gina's fast enough.

Good thing I remembered my recent traffic ticket, though, because a cop was hiding around a curve, trying to catch speeders, and I didn't see him until it was too late.

I'd thought about calling or texting Gina to make sure she kept Sue at her house. I didn't want to get there and not find Sue. But I didn't.

My heart raced and my palms felt sweaty. Funny how sometimes things pop into your head that you haven't thought about in years. For some reason I remembered a bunch of us going skiing. It was cold as hell and we took a break inside the lodge in front of this big stone fireplace. Gina, Sue, Cookie, and Lynn were there. And most of the guys who were at my house last night. It was our senior year, and Sue was seeing some guy from St. Francis Catholic High. He wasn't there.

Anyway, the fire was roaring, and it felt so good to be next to it. I remember looking over at Sue and thinking how beautiful she looked. Her cheeks and the tip of her nose were red, and she wore a striped beanie. Her blonde hair fanned out across the back of her blue ski jacket. She rubbed her hands together in front of the fire. I remember thinking how I wanted to warm her up. How I'd give anything for her to like me and not that guy from St. Francis.

Chapter 18

Sue

"Do you want something to eat?" Gina asked.

"I'm not hungry. I can't eat when I'm upset. Think I should call Tom?"

"What do you want to do?" asked Gina, sipping her tea.

"He's supposed to make me dinner tonight. Lasagna."

Gina smiled. "A man who cooks dinner for you? He's a keeper, Sues."

"Thing is, he's not coming over until 3, and I'd kind of like to see him before that."

Gina handed me her cell phone. "So call him. I'm going to get more tea."

Gina went to the kitchen to make another cup of Earl Grey. There were so many thoughts flying through my head, and they were all hitting each other, sort of like bumper cars. I'd be thinking about something and just when I'd settle on that thought I'd get hit by another thought that turned me around and pointed me in another direction. Then I'd get stuck, unable to shake the thought or fear of getting hurt—again.

I looked down at Gina's cell phone and smiled, realizing the significance of her wallpaper.

Gina had told me that Mike and she had returned to their old making-out spot in the woods. They wanted to see if they could find the old oak tree they had carved their names into more than twenty years ago.

Gina said they found the tree and that Mike, using the same pocket knife he used when they were teens, carved that day's date in the bark, below the heart.

Gina had apparently taken a photo of it afterward and saved it as her phone wallpaper. Seeing it on the phone reminded me of how sometimes love can be as strong and straight as an oak tree, but you had to plant it first.

I punched in the number I'd grown to know by heart.

Tom

I must've hit every red light there was on my way to Gina's house. If I were superstitious I'd have thought something was trying to stop me from getting there.

Just as I pulled up to the curb in front of her house, my cell phone rang. It was Gina.

"Hi, Gina."

"It's not Gina," Sue said. "I'm using her phone."

My heart thumped. I wasn't sure if I should let on that I knew anything had happened. "How was the sleepover with the girls?"

Sue sniffed. "I remembered."

"Uh, Sue," I said. "Are you inside Gina's? Cause I'm outside."

I could see Sue peek out the living room window.

"Can I come in? I think we need to talk."

Sue opened the front door, and I walked in to find Gina standing there with her purse. She bit her lower lip. "Hi, Tom. Mind if I run some errands while you two talk?"

I shook my head. "No, of course not." I held up a grocery bag containing the meat and other items that needed to be refrigerated. "Mind if I put this in your refrigerator? It's the stuff for lasagna. I don't want to let it sit in my car."

Gina took the bag and swapped cell phones with Sue. I sat on the couch beside Sue. Her face looked red and blotchy. She wrung her hands. I wanted to put my arm around her, but I couldn't tell if she wanted me to.

I look into Sue's eyes. "Do you want to talk about it?"

Sue

I sniffed. "I remember everything except right before the accident and being in the coma."

"So you remembered finding Rachel in my house?"

I nodded. "And I remember what she was wearing. The lacy thong and nipple covers with tassels. She looked so sexy and sure of herself. I just kept thinking it was happening to me all over again. And I couldn't take it. I had to get out of there."

I looked down at my lap and felt Tom's fingers beneath my chin, gently lifting it.

"I understand," he said. "But you have to know that I had no idea Rachel would ever pull a stunt like that."

"Did you see her?"

"Yes, when I got home, expecting to find you, I found her. I flipped out when I realized what had happened. Told her to leave and never come back. I even had a locksmith change the locks the next day. I'm sorry. I wish I would've remembered that Rachel had a key. It completely slipped my mind."

I raked my bottom lip with my front teeth. "It's okay. I probably overreacted. My brain was telling me one thing but my eyes were telling me something different. It's just that seeing Rachel there dressed for sex when I had gone out and bought something special to wear that night to welcome you home was too much for me. And then the way she acted. Like of course she was waiting for you, and of course you were going to screw, and of course you were going to laugh afterward at my gullibility."

I started sobbing, and Tom's arms wrapped around me. "I'm sorry," he said. "After the accident, I went to see Rachel."

I pulled back from his arms. "Why?"

"Because I wanted her to know that I personally held her responsible for your accident."

"But it wasn't Rachel's fault," I said. "She didn't make me go off the road."

"Indirectly it was her fault," Tom said. "The accident and none of this other stuff would've happened if Rachel hadn't pulled that stunt."

Tears pooled in Tom's eyes. "If I had lost you, I don't know what I would've done."

"I mean that much to you?" I asked.

"Yes," Tom said. "There's something I've been meaning to tell you."

My heart beat faster. I wondered if it was the same thing I wanted to tell him. But my cell phone rang and by the ring tone, I knew it was Chloe. She was probably wondering where I was. She had spent the night at her best friend Robin's house.

Tom

"I'd better get that," Sue said. "It's Chloe. She's probably wondering where I am."

"Chloe! What's wrong? You're crying. Where are you?"

Sue eyes widened. "Omigod. I'll be right there."

Sue looked at me. "Can you take me to the hospital?"

I jumped up from the couch. "Of course. Is Chloe all right?"

"I'm not sure. She said something about an accident and Rob driving her to the hospital."

"Who's Rob?"

"The boy down the street."

"The one whose dad was transferred here from Texas?"

"Yeah, that one. Remember I told you he's 17 and asked Chloe out? Of course Steve and I both said no and Chloe's been sulking about it ever since."

Sue ran to the bathroom, and I called Gina to tell her what was going on. She said she'd meet us at the hospital.

"If anything happens to her..." Sue shook her head.

"She's going to be okay," I told Sue. "Everything's going to be okay."

I hoped I was right.

Chapter 19

Sue

"Sorry we didn't have the chance to finish our talk," I told Tom.

"Don't worry about that. We'll talk. First things first."

We couldn't get to the hospital fast enough. The last time I'd been in the emergency room, I was the one on the gurney. And as much as I hated hospitals, I'd change places with Chloe in a second.

I swung between two extremes. One minute I was convinced Chloe was fine because she called me on her cell phone on the way to the hospital. Then the next minute I was convinced she was really hurt.

I had no idea what Chloe was doing and how she got hurt. She was supposed to be at her best friend Robin's house. What was this about Rob?

I called Steve while we were en route and couldn't reach him so I left a message. I called Robin's house, thinking that maybe Robin's mom, Tammy, would know what was going on. Chloe hadn't said anything about Robin.

Tammy answered the phone.

"Tammy, it's Sue. Is Robin there?"

"No," Tammy said. "She's out of town for the weekend."

A lump the size of a watermelon formed in my throat. "All weekend?"

"Yes," Tammy said. "She went with her cousin on a church retreat. She'll be home tomorrow. Is everything okay?"

I swallowed. "I thought Chloe was going to spend the day with her. Guess I was wrong."

"Haven't seen Chloe since last weekend. Are you sure you're okay, Sue?"

"Yeah. I have to go. I'll talk to you later."

Tom looked over at me. "What's wrong?"

"Robin's been away all weekend. Went with her cousin to a church retreat."

"But I thought you said she spent last night with Chloe and that they were spending the day together?"

I looked at Tom and mashed my lips together and let out a heavy sigh. "That's what Chloe told me."

Tom

Sue's leg shook like a rattlesnake's tail. She twisted the tissue in her hand and stared out the car window.

"I am so freaking mad right now I feel like I'm going to explode. Chloe has never done anything like this before. It's got to be that boy. Rob. He put her up to this."

"Whoa, Sue," I said. "Don't blame the boy."

"Well, of course," she said. "Of course you'd take up for the boy."

"Come on, Sue. I'm not taking any sides here. All I'm saying is that you don't know what happened, if anything. First things first. We need to make sure Chloe's okay."

She crossed her arms and sighed.

"Remember," I said. "Things aren't always what they appear to be."

Sue hit her lap with her hand. "I know. You're right. I just remember what I was doing when I was her age, and I'll kill her if she was doing what I was doing."

"I'm sure she wasn't. Not that you were bad. I mean, none of us were bad. We just did normal teen things."

"That's what I'm talking about," Sue said. "It's the normal teen things that scare me. Remember the time we all slept out in the woods?"

I smiled. I'd forgotten about the Great Sleep-out, as it had become known.

"That smile. That's what I'm talking about. I got grounded for a week, and Gina did, too, when our parents learned we'd lied to them about where we were. I told my parents I was sleeping over at Gina's and she told her parents she was sleeping over at my house. We thought we'd gotten away with it until our moms ran into each other at the grocery store."

"Uh-oh!"

"Uh-oh is right. Cost me big time. And I always thought that Chloe would never do something like that. Guess I expected too much."

I looked at her and shook my finger.

"I know. I know," she said. "Don't jump to any conclusions."

"I have to admit," I told her. "It's times like these when I'm glad I don't have kids, especially teenagers. I'm not sure my heart could handle it."

Sue smiled at me. "Don't sell yourself short, Tom. You would've made a great dad. Just look at how you are with Klondike."

"He's different. He's a dog."

"Well, don't tell him that," Sue laughed. "I'm pretty sure he thinks he's human."

It was great to see a smile on Sue's face, but it didn't hang around for long. I turned into the hospital, and the smile sprinted away.

I dropped Sue off at the emergency room doors. "I'll park the car and meet you inside."

Sue

The nurse led me to the bay Chloe was in, and when I pulled back the curtain, she burst into tears. Her hand was bandaged.

"Mom, I'm so sorry," she cried. "I did something so stupid."

I hugged her and brush her hair back off her face. "What happened?"

"I wanted vanilla ice cream, but we didn't have any. We did have ice-cream sandwiches, so I decided to cut off the chocolate wafers, only when I went to do it, the knife slipped and went into my thumb. Blood spurted everywhere, and it looked deep. So, I wrapped it in a tea towel and called Rob and he came right over. Did you see him in the waiting room when you came in?"

I shook my head. I was so relieved Chloe was okay. "You do know that most people like the chocolate wafer, right?"

My comment was meant to make Chloe laugh, but she started crying again.

"Mom," she said. "There's something else."

The curtain peeled back and in walked a tall woman with squinty eyes. A stethoscope hugged her narrow neck. "Ready to get those stitches, Chloe?"

The doctor saw me, and I held out my hand. "I'm Sue, Chloe's mother."

"I'm Dr. Morgan. I'll be stitching Chloe's thumb."

"Bet you never saw this before?" Chloe said.

Dr. Morgan smiled. "You're right. But I've seen a lot of bagel cuts. People hold the bagel in one hand while cutting it and the knife slices their palm."

Chloe squinted. "Ouch."

"But a cut from trying to remove the chocolate cookie from an ice-cream sandwich?" Dr. Morgan said. "That's definitely a new one for the books."

"Chloe," I said. "I'm going to step out. Let Tom and Aunt Gina know what's going on. I'll be right back, okay?"

Tom

Gina saw me as soon as she walked into the emergency room. We sat next to a boy who was playing a game on his cell phone.

"That's all you know?" Gina asked. "Who's Rob, anyway?"

I saw the gangly teen sit up straight and rub his neck. "Are you Rob?" I asked. "Are you the one who brought Chloe in?"

He nodded.

"So what exactly happened?"

Rob told us how Chloe cut herself, and that she'd called him because he was the closest.

"Well, thank you for bringing her in," Gina said. "I appreciate that."

I stood up and waved. "There's Sue now."

Sue came over and hugged Gina and me. "Chloe's going to be okay. Doctor says she'll need about eight stitches."

I nodded to Rob. "Rob here was just telling us what happened."

"Hi, Rob," Sue said. "Thanks for bringing Chloe in. She's going to be fine, like I said. There's no need for you to wait. We'll take her home."

"Are you sure? 'Cause I can stay."

"I'm sure. Thank you for all you did, though."

"No problem."

Rob left, and I looked at Sue. "Guess things weren't exactly as they appeared to be."

Sue smiled. "But I still have to deal with Chloe and her lying about being with Robin."

"What?" Gina said. "She wasn't with Robin?"

"I think she was with Rob," Sue said. "And that's a talk I plan to have with her later."

Sue left to go back to Chloe, and I told Gina I'd take them home.

"So did you and Sue get everything talked out?" Gina asked.

"Not quite. Chloe called, and we never finished. But our talk was going well."

"Good," Gina said. "Sue was really upset. I filled in the blanks, and that seemed to calm her a bit."

"Thanks, Gina. When are you heading back to Florida?"

"Tomorrow morning. Early flight. I should be back in a couple weeks, though. Still working through the transition. I thought I'd be able to see some of my cases through, but I can see that's not going to work."

"I'm really happy for you, Gina," I said. "Weird how everything worked out between you and Mike."

Gina patted my back. "It's going to work out between you and Sue, too. You'll see."

I smiled. "I hope."

Chapter 20

Sue

Tom dropped us off. Our plans had changed. He was going to make the lasagna at his house and bring it over later. First, he had to go to Gina's to get the groceries he'd put in her refrigerator.

"There's Dad," Chloe said as Tom pulled into the driveway.

Steve was waiting for us at the house.

"See you later," Tom said. "And if plans change, just call me."

"Hi, Dad," said Chloe, bounding into his open arms.

"How's my girl?" Steve asked.

Chloe held up her hand. "Guess Mom told you. Stupid, huh?"

Steve nodded. "Next time, when you want vanilla ice cream, don't try cutting the wafer off an ice-cream sandwich."

Steve looked at me. "How are you doing?"

"Okay. But I need some coffee."

I put on the coffee while Steve and Chloe sat down.

"Are you guys going to ground me?" Chloe asked.

"That depends," I said. "I want to know why you lied to me about being with Robin."

"Today?"

"Chloe," I said. "I talked to Tammy. I know Robin is away at a church retreat with her cousin. All weekend."

Chloe covered her face with her hands and started to cry. "I'm so sorry, Mom. Dad. It's just that you guys wouldn't let me go out with Rob and I really, really, really wanted to go out with him. I'm the only one of my friends who isn't allowed to date. Even Robin can date. And I feel like a baby when everyone at the lunch table talks about dating, so I decided to go out with Rob, but I swear that nothing happened, not even a kiss. We just went to the movies, and then he brought me home and he didn't come inside. I swear."

Steve looked at me, then hugged Chloe. I knew I was going to have to play the heavy.

"Chloe," I said. "I'm disappointed. I'm disappointed you lied. I've told you over and over again that the worst thing you can do to me is lie. You've broken the trust I had in you."

Steve shifted in his seat. I could tell I was making him uncomfortable, too.

"I'm sorry, Mom." The sobs shifted into high gear. "I promise. I won't ever do it again."

"I'm going to count on you keeping that promise."

Chloe nodded. "Am I grounded?"

I crossed my arms. "I'll think about it."

"Hey kiddo," Steve said. "I know it's not your night to be with me, but I'm feeling like some daddy/daughter time." Steve looked at me. "You okay with that, Sue? I'll drop her off at school tomorrow."

I looked at Chloe. "It's up to Chloe."

Tom

I was making the lasagna when Sue called. There was a change in plans. Turns out Chloe was spending the night with her dad so Sue was coming to my house for dinner—and to finish the discussion we started earlier.

I put the lasagna in the oven and then jumped in the shower. I remembered the last time Sue was at my house. We had great shower sex. I missed making love to her. I'd never felt this way about anyone before, and it scared me a little. It scared me to think that I could care about someone this much. It was a lot easier when I was more concerned about my life and my needs than someone else's. Guess that's why they call it love.

Klondike barked when he heard Sue's car pull into the driveway.

"I brought dessert," said Sue, getting out of the car with a bakery box.

"Let me guess. Tiramisu."

She playfully slapped my shoulder. "How'd you guess?"

"Figured you'd want to keep the Italian theme going."

Sue sat the box on the kitchen table. "So what do you need me to do?"

"The lasagna's not quite done. I have the salad made. We might as well enjoy a glass of wine."

I poured the wine, and we went into the living room.

"So, everything go okay with Chloe?"

Sue sighed. "Yeah, I guess. She lied because she wanted to go out with Rob. She said nothing happened, not even a kiss, and when he dropped her off, he didn't come inside the house."

"Do you believe her?"

"Yes, I do. But I told her I was very disappointed that she lied. I hate liars. She knows that. I'm still undecided if I should punish her. On the one hand, I want to, and on the other, I was thinking about cutting her a break."

"What's Steve think?"

"Hell, he's useless. When it comes to Chloe she can do nothing wrong, even though he agreed she was too young to date."

"Does he still feel that way?"

"I'm not sure. I guess it's a conversation I'm going to have to have with him sooner or later."

"You're probably right."

Sue slipped off her shoes. "Can we talk about something else?"

"Absolutely," I said. "What do you want to talk about?"

Sue

"Can we continue our talk from earlier?"

Tom smiled. "Do you remember where we stopped?"

"You told me you went to see Rachel after my accident. And you told Rachel you held her personally responsible for what happened. That if I wouldn't have found her at your house, I wouldn't have been mad and we wouldn't have gotten into a fight and the accident would've never occurred."

Tom ran his fingers through his hair. "Do you remember what you asked me?"

I did remember but I didn't want to repeat it. It was like having a gift and hoping that it's a particular thing but being anxious to open it in case it isn't.

I shrugged.

Tom's blue-gray eyes swallowed mine. "I think you know," he smiled. "You asked me if you meant that much to me."

My lips trembled, and I could feel my body begin to quiver for Tom's touch.

Tom's eyes stayed glued to mine. "And I told you I had something I've been meaning to tell you for a while."

I gulped.

Tom's eyes became glassy. "I love you, Sue. I think I've always loved you, ever since seventh-grade science class."

I smiled.

"And I don't want to lose you. Ever."

I couldn't stop the tears from coming. This gorgeous man loved me, really loved me. And I knew at that moment that no man had ever loved me the way Tom did. It was so weird, but I could feel it. And it was something I'd never felt before. I thought I'd loved Steve, and I'm sure that on some level I did. But it was different with Tom. Just different.

"I love everything about you," he continued. "The quirky things you do, like putting notes on the underside of the toilet seat. I love the way you look first thing in the morning and the way you take a Q-tip and stick it in your mouth and wipe off mascara that gets on your eyelid when you apply your makeup."

I sniffed and dabbed my eyes with a tissue.

"I love the way you laugh at my jokes even when they're lame, and the way you make me feel when I'm lying next to you. Christ, I miss that."

Tom

I brushed Sue's hair off her face, and we kissed hard and deep. I wanted her so badly.

Her breath tickled my neck, and she nibbled on my ear. "I love you," she whispered.

I pulled back. Now I was the one with tears. "You're not saying that just because I said it, are you?"

Sue shook her head. "I've wanted to tell you for a while. But I was scared, scared to love someone again, afraid that I might get hurt."

"I'd never hurt you," I said. "I've waited my whole life to find someone like you, and now that I have, I never want to let you go."

We kissed again, and I felt Sue's hand slide up my thigh and over my crotch. She tugged at my zipper, all the while kissing me. "You drive me crazy."

Our hands were all over each other. Ripping off shirts, pulling down pants. Sue's bare chest was against mine and ... Shit!

The timer on the oven went off.

"The lasagna's done," I said.

"Forget about the lasagna," said Sue, pulling me toward her. "I'd much rather have you for dinner."

"But it might burn."

"I don't care," she said. "I'm burning."

"Tell you what. You race upstairs. I'll take the lasagna out of the oven and meet you in bed."

Sue grabbed her shirt and bra and took off for my bed, and I took off for the kitchen.

Chapter 21

Sue

I ran upstairs and went to the bathroom. I swished a swig of mouthwash around in my mouth. I was naked in bed by the time Tom walked into the bedroom.

I watched as he dropped his boxers, and I could see he was just as excited as I was. When he climbed into bed, we picked up where we'd left off on the couch. I felt his lips on my neck, planting a trail of kisses down my chest, taking each nipple in his mouth, sucking gently, going lower and lower. I moaned. "Please. Stop teasing me."

"I'm not teasing you," he whispered, spreading my legs with his hands. "I just want to take it slowly, build your desire."

"I'm there," I moaned. "Please."

And then I felt him enter me, so easily. My body arched up, and I grabbed his back.

"Do you want to be on top?" he asked.

He rolled over, and I was on top and he was so hard and so deep, and I came multiple times. I rolled over and he was on top, and I matched his rhythm and our bodies were one once again and I had another orgasm, coming at the same time as Tom and feeling like I'd never felt before.

"God, Sue," Tom said. "You're incredible."

He lay beside me, slipping his arm around me and pulling me as close to him as he could. I lay my face on his chest, next to his heart. It was still beating fast. "I wish this would last forever," I said.

Tom kissed the top of my head. "There's no reason it can't. I know I'm not going to be the one to walk away."

"Me, neither. I think I've finally found the love of my life. I'm just sorry it didn't happen sooner."

Tom

Sue and I fell asleep and when we woke up, the lasagna was cold. We decided to save it for the next day. Sue would take it home, heat it up for dinner, and I'd take the salad to her house after work, and we'd eat with Chloe.

"And bring Klondike, too," Sue said. "Or Chloe will be very disappointed."

We grabbed bowls of cereal and went back to bed, finding each other again and again.

"I'm going to be sore in the morning," Sue said.

"Do you want me to stop?"

Sue pulled me back to her. "Never."

I couldn't remember the last time I'd made love so many times in a row. To be honest, I kind of surprised myself. At my age, I wouldn't have thought I'd be able to perform. But it wasn't a problem.

I felt so comfortable with Sue. With other women I've been with, I was self-conscious about having only one testicle. They always said they understood about the cancer, but I always felt as if I had a defect. With Sue, it was different. She actually made me feel sexy, not ashamed or embarrassed. It felt great not to feel like I wasn't whole. If a guy can feel beautiful, Sue made me feel that way. Strange, I know. But that's how she made me feel.

Sue had asked me if she had to have a breast removed, would that change the way I felt about her. Of course I said no.

"It's no different for me when it comes to you having one testicle," she said. "It's part of who you are, what you've been through, the struggle you've faced and the mountain you've climbed. You fought cancer and you won. So what if you have only one testicle? There's more to a man than what hangs between his legs. A lot more."

I will always love Sue for saying that. Talk about feeling like you never quite measure up. She made me feel like one of the sexiest men in the world. I loved her for that.

Sue

Gina texted me the next day while I was at work.

Everything go okay last night with Tom?

It was perfect.

Great. Call me later.

Will do.

It was hard concentrating on work, and it wasn't only because I was tired. It's true, I hadn't slept much the night before. But the real reason for my lack of concentration was Tom. I kept thinking about last night and the incredible sex we had. But more importantly, how close I felt to him. I'd never eaten cereal in bed with a man before. And I'd never been with someone who made me laugh so much. He could turn something serious into something funny as quick as you could flip a light switch. Me? I could never think that fast on my feet. I admired that about him.

At work, I'd remember one of his one-liners and smile. Nancy caught me smiling more than once.

"What's all the smiles about?" she'd asked.

I shrugged my shoulders.

"Must involve a man. No one smiles as much as you do unless there's a man involved."

Chloe had texted me during lunch, and I told her Tom was coming to dinner. She asked if she could invite Rob. I think she felt that if I got to know him I might feel differently about the whole dating thing. I knew there'd be plenty of food, and I thought maybe Chloe had a point. Maybe I should give the kid a chance. Maybe he wasn't out to just sleep with my daughter. Maybe he was someone like Tom.

Tom said it was no big deal. He'd just add to the salad and make sure there was plenty. And he thought Chloe might have a point.

"I'm not taking sides," he had said. "But what would it hurt getting to know Rob better? I see his name in the paper all of the time. The kid's a good ball player."

I hadn't even realized he played baseball. Guess there were a lot of things I didn't know.

Tom

"So, Rob," I said, when we started to eat. "From what I read in the paper, it sounds like the season's going pretty well."

He nodded. "Yes, sir. It's been good. I was worried when we moved here that I wouldn't get any pitching time. But as it turned out, the coach has really been using me. Kind of feel bad for Josh, though. He used to pitch all of the time. Now, coach mixes it up a bit."

"Great lasagna, Tom," Chloe said.

"Thanks."

"Mom, can Tom make dinner every night?"

Sue smiled. "Am I that bad of a cook?"

"No offense, Mom, but you're a pretty bad cook. Except pancakes. Pancakes you can do."

We laughed.

"It is really good," said Rob, reaching for another piece of Italian bread.

Sue sipped her wine. "Any college plans yet, Rob?"

Rob cleared his throat. "Yes, ma'am. I have a few I'm thinking about."

Rob was way more polite than any kid his age I knew. Everything was Ma'am and Sir and thank you and no thank you. I could tell by the way Sue smiled and how her body relaxed more and more through dinner that she liked Rob. And I knew I'd get her full report later.

Looking around the table, I suddenly felt like an old man. Seeing Chloe and Rob reminded me of Sue and me when we were their age. They had their entire lives ahead of them, and along with that would come the good and bad, the ups and downs, and the wisdom that comes from having navigated through it all.

I looked across the table at Sue, and I couldn't help feeling like I had found my home. It's weird how it hit me, like an unexpected gift that when you unwrap it, you find way more than you'd expected.

Love and family. A sense of belonging.

And I was happy. And I knew that Sue was, too.

Sue's Classmates

BRAD (YEARBOOK POST)

Sue, to a hot chick that I would have liked to have gotten to know better. Take care of yourself.

Brad

Gina's right. Brad always thought he was God's gift to women. I about died when I saw him at our 20th year reunion. His bald head looked like a pig's ass without the crack. And his gut hung over his belt. Definitely not one of the guys who got better looking with age. Karma sucks. That's all I have to say. Serves him right for being such a jerk to every girl he ever dated.

KAREN (YEARBOOK POST)

Sue, to a really flipped-out chick that I met in eighth grade. Remember all the fun we had in gym class and take care of that special someone. Keep your personality and good looks and you'll go far.

Love, Karen

Karen was an amazing athlete. Most of us thought for sure she'd go to college and become a gym teacher. She ended up getting pregnant our senior year. She married the guy but it didn't last. She and her daughter, Sarah, lived with her parents. They helped raise Sarah while Karen worked her way through school, first earning a marketing degree and later an MBA. Karen met Mia, her partner, while studying for her MBA.

They make a great couple. And they have the most adorable little boy. Karen got pregnant, using Mia's egg and donor sperm. He looks just like Mia, same almond-shaped eyes and shiny black hair.

It was great to reconnect with Karen and Mia at our high school reunion. I think Karen felt good that we all accepted Mia, and that her being gay was no big deal.

TOM (YEARBOOK POST)

Sue, to a really nice and good looking girl I met in seventh grade earth science class. I hope to see you around this summer. Good luck in college and take care of yourself.

AFA, Tom

Even today Tom still brings up that earth science class and how he did most of the worm dissection. I'm not going to deny it. Dissecting a worm totally grossed me out. Just thinking about it makes me want to barf— even today. It never surprised me that he excelled in the sciences. I wasn't surprised when he went to college to become a pharmacist, especially because he loved chemistry so much.

Mom was cleaning out her basement a few years ago and came across a box filled with old school notebooks. There was a yellow spiral notebook with Earth Science written in black marker on the front. I paged through it and couldn't help but smile at the drawings I'd made of the different parts of the worm. Gosh, the worm sketches took me back. I swear I could smell the formaldehyde, that's how vivid the memories were.

I can't believe that Tom and I got together. I always thought he was a great guy. Maybe a little on the nerdy side. But not nerdy nerdy. More like cool nerdy.

And, unlike Brad, Tom definitely got better looking with age. Not that he was ever bad looking; he wasn't. He was definitely above average, especially with his cute dimples. That sort of put him over the top. But today, whoa! Let's just say I'm glad he's mine, and I don't plan on giving him up. Talk about chemistry, we have it!

DIANE (YEARBOOK POST)

Sue,

Years from now when you clean out your closet and find this yearbook, I hope you open it and remember me and all the fun we had. Thanks for being such a great friend. I'll miss marching band and the crazy bus rides home from the parades. We sure had some wild times! Thanks for always listening to me and giving me good advice. I hope we keep in touch and that you get everything you want.

Love, Diane

I haven't thought about marching band or the bus rides home from parades in a long time. Diane's right. We had some really crazy times. Once, we sneaked vodka in a water bottle onto the bus and passed it around on the ride home. Because we were seniors, we always got the back seats. By the time we got back to the school, we were all feeling a little buzzed—and a lot sick.

I played the flute, and Diane played the tuba. I stunk. I never practiced. Diane, on the other hand, was really good. She became a music teacher at our high school and replaced the band director we had. I bet Diane never lets the kids get away with the stuff we got away with.

COOKIE (YEARBOOK POST)

Sue, to one of my good friends who's one of the best cheerleaders at our school—and a great gymnast. Wish I could handle those uneven bars like you. I look like a flying hippo! Thanks for always being there for me when I needed someone to talk to. Remember all the fun we had at Jeremy's and stay cool and keep in touch.

Love, Cookie

One word. Hilarious. That's what Cookie is and has always been. I could be having the crappiest day and feel like crying and Cookie would say something and make me double over laughing so hard I had tears in my eyes. Like bright sunshine on an overcast day, she can burn away the gray and douse you in warmth in seconds. She's one of those people who you totally enjoy being around. I wish I had her sense of humor and her ability to make others laugh at the most stupid, everyday stuff. What a gift.

I love that she always does her own thing and never cares what others think. In high school, she went through some pretty wild clothing phases. Some of the girls made fun of her, but I thought it was great that she did her own thing. Personally, I wouldn't have been caught dead in some of the outfits she wore, but I admired her for having the guts to dress differently and the strength to stand on her own. I don't know too many people who embrace their silly side and aren't afraid of being goofy. I'm glad we've kept in touch over the years.

She had a crappy first marriage, but she seems happy in her second marriage and I'm happy that she's happy. Funny, though, her twin girls aren't anything like her. They're tall and thin and gorgeous—and definitely conformists. Maybe that's a good thing, though. Three Cookies might've been a bit too much.

MARGARET (YEARBOOK POST)

Sue, I'm really glad I got to know you even better this year. Don't forget all the fun we had in cheerleading. You have more energy than anyone I know. Just watching you makes me tired. You have a lot going for you, and I wish you much happiness.

Luv ya, Maggie

Maggie isn't married—yet. I think she was too busy pursuing her career. She's a very successful businesswoman, having climbed her way up Dye Works Inc. where she is now general manager and vice president.

One of the things I love most about Maggie is that she gives back. Despite her success and wealth, she's never forgotten where she came from and how hard it was climbing to the top.

She's never liked the limelight, so I'm sure all of the photos in the newspaper of her giving oversized checks to charities make her uncomfortable.

ELLEN (YEARBOOK POST)

Tig,

To a very special friend who always seems to be there just in case someone needs her. You are a super person, and I hope we stay close. Never forget senior hook-off day and how we almost got caught swimming in the quarry. Stay the way you are (your sweetness, personality and looks) and you will go far. I hope things work out with you and Ron. You make a great couple.

Love, El

Ellen was always a lot of fun. And she was a great cook. She went to culinary school and became a chef. She loved baking and was forever trying new recipes.

Whenever it was one of our birthdays, Ellen would make a special treat and bring it to school and we'd have it at lunch. It was such a sweet thing to do, and something we all looked forward to. Ellen made these killer brownies with chocolate chips in them. They were so moist and whenever it was my birthday, she made them because she knew how much I loved them. One year for Christmas, I bought a plain white apron and had all of the girls sign it using fabric markers. When she opened the apron, Ellen cried. I wonder if she still has that apron?

BECKY (YEARBOOK POST)

Sue,

To a great friend who's always on the go. You definitely are just like Tigger. (Smiles) Thank you for always listening to me. I really appreciate all you've done for me this past year. I will miss you when I go into the Air Force. I hope we keep in touch and that years from now we can laugh about all of the crazy things we did. Keep that special smile and that way of making others feel important.

A.V.G.F.A. Love, Becky

I wish I would've kept in touch with Becky. After she went into the Air Force and I went to college, we drifted apart. Sad when you think about it. We had been friends for a long time. In fact, Becky was the one who introduced me to Spin the Bottle. We played it once in her garage and her mom caught us, but not before I got a kiss from Kurt Wallace. It was an okay kiss. It would've been better if his breath wasn't so stinky. He smelled like my grandpa does after he eats raw garlic.

Kurt moved the following year, and we were all glad he wasn't around to play Spin the Bottle because nobody wanted to kiss him. I wonder whatever became of Kurt, and if he still has the stinky breath.

GINA (YEARBOOK POST)

Sues, To my best friend in the whole wide world. God, we've been through so much together. I don't know what I'd do without you. Remember all the fun we had cheering over the years and the bus rides home from games. (Remember the time Brad mooned a cop from the bus window?) Thanks for always being there for me and for always telling me the truth, even when I didn't want to hear it. I hope we stay sisters forever! Promise me that when we go away to college, things won't change. I'm always here if you need to talk, and I hope that you and Ron last a long time.

Love you always, Gina

Gina. My best friend, killer ass attorney, godmother to my child, and all-around fabulous person. I don't know what I would've done without Gina. Not only did she help me when I found my husband screwing our neighbor, but she's been a wonderful aunt to Chloe. I'm so excited that she's moving home and that after all these years, she's reunited with the love of her life. YAY!

As for Ron, by now you know it didn't work out. Chloe picked up my yearbook the other day and was reading what everyone wrote. She asked me about Ron. And about the "crazy and wild" bus rides home from parades and games. And about senior hook-off day. I would've preferred that she hadn't read that! God, I really am becoming my mother!

JEREMY (YEARBOOK POST)

Sue, to a really cool girl who is a lot of fun to be around. Remember the good times we had and the wild parties. Take care of yourself and good luck in college.

Love, Bean

Jeremy sure knew how to throw a party. And he's right, they were wild. After high school, Jeremy went to college in the Midwest where he played basketball. He married a girl he met in dental school and joined his dad's dental practice. His best friend is Mike, Gina's boyfriend.

Jeremy is still as goofy as ever, and he still has wild parties. In fact, he lives in the house he grew up in. When his parents downsized, Jeremy bought it. Jeremy's dad used to be my dentist, but after he retired I found another dentist. I used the excuse that I wanted to go to a dentist close to my work. The truth was that the thought of Jeremy digging around in my mouth made me gag a little. I'm sure he's a great dentist. It's just that I can't get certain images out of my mind. Sort of how I can't eat venison because I see Bambi every time I take a bite. What can I say? I'm weird, I know.

MIKE (YEARBOOK POST)

Tigger, to one of the best girls in our senior class. Thanks for being such a good friend to Gina and me. I'll never forget all of the double dates we went on and the crazy things we did. Take care of yourself, and I know you won't let any guy push you around.

Later, Mike

I've always adored Mike and was so upset when Gina broke up with him our senior year. Of course, now I know why and it all makes sense. But back then, not so much. They were always great together—the couple everyone voted the most likely to marry.

I wish Gina would've told me about the rape. I can't help but think how different things could've been. Mike was devastated when she broke up with him out of the blue. I've never seen a guy so torn up over a girl. I used to think how great it would be if someone loved me even half as much as Mike loved Gina.

But you can't undo the past. Mike went to college on a baseball scholarship and eventually married a girl he met there. Although the marriage didn't last, their divorce was very friendly. They had one child, Jack, and both he and Lisa always made sure he came first. Now Jack will be getting another sibling (Lisa remarried and has a baby girl.). Gina says he's not too wild about another crying baby, but my guess is that he'll be just fine.

I keep thinking about Gina's baby and whether it will be a girl or a boy. I'm secretly hoping for a girl, but

I know that it doesn't matter to Gina and Mike, as long as the baby's healthy. But Gina has always wanted to have a daughter and name her Daisy. I hope she gets that chance.

KEITH (YEARBOOK POST)

Sue, to a girl who's constantly on the go. Never forget all the fun we had in Hoffman's class and thanks for all the times you kept me awake. Good luck in college and don't break too many guys' hearts.

AFA, Keith

Keith never did his homework. He was one of those kids who got A's without even trying. I hated that about him. Me? I had to work my ass off to get a B.

I can't believe that Keith and his wife, who he met in college, have five kids. Two sets of twin girls and one boy! Wow! At least they don't have to pay for eye exams! Turned out Keith became an eye doctor and joined his dad's practice.

He's definitely one of those guys who got better looking with age. He kind of grew into his big ears and narrow nose, and if I saw him on the street, I'd definitely look twice.

RON (YEARBOOK POST)

Sue, to the best girlfriend a guy could have. I'm really glad we met in the hallway after the game. Thanks for always listening to me when I go off about things and thanks for everything you do for me, which is a lot. I can't wait to spend more time with you this summer. I wish we were going to the same college but I know that we'll see each other when we come home. I love you, and I want what we have to work out.

Love, Ron

Ron was my first real love, and I thought we'd be together forever. I met him in the hallway after a basketball game. I lost my virginity to him the summer before we started college. It was the first year I didn't go on vacation with my family. I helped run the recreation program at the community park and couldn't get off work. Ron came over after work one night and we ended up in my white canopy bed.

To be honest, the first time we did it I was disappointed. The way Gina and some of my other girlfriends talked, I expected it was going to be earth shattering. Turned out it hurt way more than I thought it would, and I never did have an orgasm—not once the entire time Ron and I were together. In fact, I pretended I did just so Ron wouldn't feel bad.

A couple of years later I met this guy in college. Matt was only the second guy I'd ever slept with, but I'll never forget the first orgasm I had happened in his dorm room. I'm like, so THIS is what all the fuss is about. Yeah, baby. Bring it on. And he did. Lots of times.

FRED (YEARBOOK POST)

Sue, to a girl I knew for a few years and am glad I didn't know longer. Ha. Ha. Be good and keep out of trouble.

Fred

Fred always was a comedian. Like Cookie, he had a natural gift for making people laugh. And a lot of the times he made himself the target. I always thought he did this because he was afraid other people would make fun of him so he made fun of himself first, sort of taking the wind out of their sails.

He also had the loudest and lowest belch of anyone I knew. That's how he got the nickname Foghorn, which he hated. You could be on one side of the school building and he could be on the other side and you'd hear his belch echo through the maze of hallways.

LYNN (YEARBOOK POST)

Sue, to a really great girl I met in 7th grade. You're a terrific friend and really fun to be around. You're always moving and always smiling! Never forget all of the games we cheered at. And thanks for always being there for me. You're a good listener, and I appreciate all of the times you spent listening to me and all my guy drama. Keep up those good looks. I know I'll never forget you so keep in touch!

Love, Lynn

I never knew anyone who was as good as Lynn when it came to planning events. She was our class president and voted the most likely to succeed. She's an events planner at a country club and has always planned all of our class reunions. Somehow she makes it seem so effortless, and I'm sure it's not.

One time Lynn and I were out partying, and she got drunk. The problem was that she was sleeping overnight at my house and I had to get her in my house and past my dad, which wasn't easy. I think Dad knew something was up, but he ignored us when we walked past him. The next morning, Dad asked Lynn how she felt and she mumbled that she wasn't feeling too hot. And I swear there was a smirk on my dad's face.

JIM (YEARBOOK POST)

Sue, to one of the neatest chicks I've ever met with good looks and a great personality. Good luck in everything you do.

A.V.G.F.A.   Love, Jim

Jim lived down the street. He was a couple of years older than me but we played together all of the time when we were kids. After high school, he went in the Navy. I'd see him every once in a while when he came home on leave. He married someone he met in the service, and they live in Virginia. Mom told me he has a couple of boys, and they sound like they're a chip off the old block. Jim was always a daredevil. I think he had more broken bones than anyone I know.

When he was four, he was playing at my house and jumped off my top bunk. He ended up with a fracture! After that, Mom didn't let us play in my bedroom.

PATRICK (YEARBOOK POST)

Sue, to a nice looking girl who got a lot prettier since 2nd grade. Good luck in the future.

Love, Pat

Pat always made me smile. He had this goofy grin and a great sense of humor. His ears stuck straight out, and the kids teased him and called him Dopey. I told him they were just jealous, that his ears made him special. But he cried anyway. I remember asking him what he wanted for Christmas one year and he said, "New ears." Eventually he had an operation so his ears laid flat against his head. He was so happy after that. But I kind of missed his old ears.

Tess & Jeremy

Chapter 1

Jeremy

I never saw it coming. I thought Tess was happy. I thought I'd given her a good life. I didn't know she was checking out until she was half way out the door. And I hoped I could stop her before she closed it for good.

It started with little things. Like I noticed she was losing weight. Not that she was fat, but after a couple of kids she had more around the middle than when we were married fourteen years ago. I still thought she was as sexy as hell. And I told her that. But I could feel her pulling away more each day.

I couldn't figure out what I was doing wrong. I tried complimenting her more, but that only seemed to piss her off. "You're just saying that to make me feel better," she'd say.

She complained I didn't do enough around the house, but when I tried doing more, it was never right. And sex? Don't even get me started. I've never been priest material. When I met Tess in dental school, we screwed every chance we got. We even did it on the dental chair once!

But now? Now I'm lucky to get it once a month, and I'm horny as hell. I'm trying to be understanding, give her some space. I thought maybe she was in some kind of funk. But when my buddy Keith told me about his wife, Kris, and him doing the deed for 31 days straight, I became worried. And then when he told me about Kris dabbing chocolate five different places on her body and him having to find the five places and lick off the chocolate while blindfolded, I *really* became worried. My sex life—er marriage—was in a definite nosedive, and I'll be damned if I knew how to stop it from crashing.

When I came home from work, I found Tess in the kitchen making dinner. "How was your day?"

She didn't look up from slicing carrots for the salad she was making. "Same as yesterday."

I grabbed a beer from the refrigerator. "I thought you had parent visitation at Katie's school."

"I did."

"How'd that go?"

"Fine."

I sipped my beer. "Not in the mood to talk?"

Tess scooped up the carrot slices and tossed them into the salad bowl. "I want to talk, but you don't want to hear what I have to say."

"Come on, Tess. That's not fair. I always listen to what you have to say."

This time she looked up at me, her twitching eyes boring into mine. "Okay. I want to go back to work."

I wiped my mouth with the back of my hand. "But we talked about this."

Tess narrowed her eyes. "You talked. I tried to talk, but you didn't listen."

"I just don't see why you want to get a job when you don't have to. You can golf at the country club anytime you want. Go shopping every day if you want. You have more time for yourself now than you ever did with both kids in school and not needing you as much. Most women would kill to have your life."

Tess threw the dish towel she'd been holding onto the counter. "You just don't get it, do you? I'm not like most women!"

I drank the last sip of my beer as she flew up the stairs. I heard our bedroom door slam shut.

Tess

I knew I had to calm down. Jeremy made my blood boil, and I didn't want to get into another fight. It seemed as if that's all we did anymore. Fight, fight, fight! And fight some more! I couldn't remember the last time Jeremy came home from work and we had a normal conversation. Usually within five minutes of him getting home our conversation deteriorates into a screaming match. I was beginning to feel as if I lived in a war zone, and all of the yelling wasn't good for the kids. Just this morning Katie asked if her dad and I were getting a divorce. Of course I said no, but I found myself thinking about the possibility more and more. I just couldn't make Jeremy understand I wanted to go back to work.

When the kids were younger and needed me more, I had no problem not working outside the home. In fact, I enjoyed the stay-at-home momminess and everything that came with it—story time at the library and days spent at the park or pool. But they're in third and fifth grade, old enough to walk home from the bus stop, fix an afternoon snack and do their homework with the help of a babysitter.

I loved being Katie's and John's mom, but I wanted more than to be their mom. I wanted a career I could feel good about. I wanted the pre-mom me, and damn if I could get that through Jeremy's brick brain. I couldn't seem to make him understand I needed to have something that made me feel good about myself, something outside the family and home that was all mine. I wasn't exactly sure what it would be, but I want to explore and find out.

And the more Jeremy resisted, the more I pulled away. I focused on other things that made me feel good—like getting in shape. At least *that* was something I had control over. And I had no interest in having sex with him. I felt so misunderstood and alone. I'd be willing to go to counseling, but I wasn't sure Jeremy would. He didn't like other people knowing our business.

I heard a knock on the door. I knew it was Jeremy. "Go away!"

Jeremy cracked open the door. "Can I come in?"

"Only if you'll listen. If you're not going to listen, don't bother."

He walked in and closed the door.

"So, you really think getting a job will make you happier?"

I clenched my teeth. "That's what I've been saying."

Jeremy sat down on the bed next to me. "My mom didn't work, and she was happy."

I stared into the dark eyes that once melted me in seconds. "Well, I'm not your mom."

"People might think I'm not a good provider?"

"Jesus! Are you serious? You're really worried about that shit! Get over it. I don't give a damn what anyone thinks. This isn't about you being a good provider. This is about me wanting a job so I feel useful and good about myself."

"But what if the kids get sick?"

"Your mom has always offered to help out anytime. You just never wanted to ask her."

Jeremy rubbed his neck. "Well, we sure can't continue fighting like this. Even the dog crawls under the sofa whenever we're in the same room."

"Look, Jeremy. I've decided I'm going to get a job whether you like it or not. Now, I'm really hoping you'll support me. But if you don't, I'll do it anyway."

"But the wash and cleaning and all the other stuff."

"What about it?"

"Who's going to do it if you work?"

"Guess we'll have to do like most married couples and split the jobs."

Jeremy punched the bed. "I work long days at the office, and the last thing I want to do is come home and make dinner."

"Then find someone else to make it for you."

I stormed out of the bedroom and went to the kitchen to finish making the kids dinner. As far as Jeremy was concerned, he could just go fuck himself. I've had it.

Jeremy

Damn Tess. I don't want my life to change. I like coming home from work and having dinner on the table. I like knowing the kids are taken care of, the house is clean and the laundry done. And the last thing I want is for her to change all that. I did an informal poll at work and every woman in my dental office said if given the chance, she'd choose staying home over working. But no! Not my wife.

My best friend, Mike, suggested marriage counseling. But I'm not crazy about sharing all this personal stuff with a therapist. Besides, I think we can fix what's wrong ourselves. I suggested to Tess she volunteer more at the school, but she says if she volunteers anymore the teachers will get sick of seeing her.

When we married, Tess was a graphic artist for an advertising company. Later, she became art director for a regional women's magazine. She loved that job, but decided to stay home when we had John. Her mother had always worked, and Tess said she always envied the kids whose moms were waiting for them at the end of the school day. She was happy for a while, but little by little, I could see she was becoming restless. Katie's birth changed things for a while, but now we've come full circle.

I went downstairs to see if I could help with dinner, but Tess and the kids were already eating. Katie, who looked like a miniature Tess with black hair and violet eyes, looked up at me. "Why do you and Mom fight all the time?"

I patted her on the head before sitting down. "We don't, sweetie."

"Do, too," John chimed in. "We heard you. Upstairs."

Katie nodded. "Yeah, Mom said 'Jesus' and we learned in Sunday school you're not supposed to say that when you're mad. You're supposed to say it only when you pray."

I looked at Tess who was mashing her lips together so hard they were turning blue.

"I'm sorry, Katie," I said. "You're right. We shouldn't have said that."

"And you shouldn't have said 'damn' either," John added.

I looked at John. "That, too."

Tess and I didn't talk much during dinner. Mostly we listened to the kids talk about their day.

Tess

When Katie mentioned she overheard me say Jesus, I realized the kids were tuned into what had been going on far more than I realized.

"How was your practice spelling test today?" I asked Katie during dinner.

She jabbed a carrot slice with her fork. "Okay. I got one wrong."

"Which one?"

"Vocal. I put two *l*'s at the end."

John pointed to me and Jeremy. "That's what you guys were when you were upstairs. Vocal."

Katie smiled. "Thanks, John. I can use that when I write my sentences. Mom and Dad are vocal when they fight."

I coughed. "Oh, Katie. I'm sure you can come up with a better sentence than that."

Katie shook her head. "I like that sentence. It's perfect."

I looked across the table at Jeremy, and he rolled his eyes. "Remember tomorrow night, Tess. We're going to Tom's house for dinner."

Katie rubbed her hands together. "Is Cassie going to babysit us?"

I nodded. I was actually looking forward to seeing Gina and Sue and the other girls. I really liked them, and I thought they might be able to give me some advice on how to handle Jeremy.

I'd been going to the gym a lot lately, and the manager, who's also a kick-ass instructor, asked if I'd ever considered teaching classes. I hadn't, but the more I thought about it, the more interested I became.

What people are saying about
Class Acts: Gina and Mike

"The highs and lows keep you reading and anxious to see what's next."

"Wonderfully relatable characters whose lives are forever altered by the choice of silence."

"A story of friendship, love and redemption, this book will grab you from the beginning and leave you wanting more."

"This is a perfect vacation read, once you start you won't put it down until you're finished!"

"It will make you laugh and make you cry, and realize the importance of friends and family - and how a secret can change your life."

"Buffy Andrews draws you in with action from the very start of this novel."

"The characters feel like old friends and will bring the reader back to their high school days."

"A quick page turner, you won't be able to put this book down."

"This is a great story about the vagaries of life, but also about the redemptive and healing power of love."

"If you love a romance about second chances, with characters that will break your heart only to put it back together again … pick up a copy of "Gina and Mike" from the Class Acts Series."

"I was hooked immediately on the characters and what was going to happen next. I hope that there will be more to the series …"

"The book is riveting and engaging as vivid memories of high-school and first love spill off the pages and into your soul."

"I loved this book! After tragedies and heartache, Gina and Mike try to rekindle their love after 20 years apart. The highs and lows keep you reading and anxious to see what's next. Great story!"

"I look forward to each new book in this series. What a clever idea to take a yearbook and form stories around students and what happened to them and who they became."

"Buffy Andrews's works are worth taking a look at! What a great storyteller! I'm a Buffy fan!"

"This book made me feel like I was back in high school re-living my youth through the characters. I would recommend this book to my friends."

"The characters are believable and poignant. They make tough decisions, grapple with regret and try to make the most of their situations. As someone happily married to my high school sweetheart, I love how it shows first loves can last a lifetime."

"The characters are very real and engage the reader from the beginning."

"This book was a page turner that I just couldn't put down. I can't wait for more novels to come!!!"

"I can't wait to read more from this author!"

Acknowledgments

There are so many people I'd like to thank for their continued love and support.

God, who is always with me.

My sisters Dawn Beakler, Cindy Andrews and Tania Nade, who keep all my secrets, share all my dreams and hold my heart in their hands.

My sons, Zach and Micah, who remind me of all that is good in this world.

And, lastly, my husband, Tom, who loves me and encourages me to follow my dreams, even when that means spending less time with him.

Facebook
www.facebook.com/AuthorBuffyAndrews

Twitter
https://twitter.com/buffyandrews

Goodreads
www.goodreads.com/author/show/
7113753.Buffy_Andrews

Website
www.authorbuffyandrews.com

Amazon
www.amazon.com/Buffy-
Andrews/e/B00EO7F1IG

About the Author

Buffy Andrews is a best-selling Amazon author of women's fiction and thriller and suspense novels. Her best-seller credits include *The Perfect Husband*, *The Moment Keeper*, *The Christmas Violin* and *A Year of Second Chances*. A two-time Pulitzer judge, she was a journalist for nearly thirty years before starting Andrews Creative Concepts. She specializes in creating viral interactive content and marketing strategies for clients worldwide. She lives in southcentral Pennsylvania with her husband, Tom.

*Vote for the Class Acts couple
you'd like to read about next...*

Kris and Keith

Cookie and Harry

Maggie and James

Karen and Mia

Cast your vote at http://bit.ly/35zdR9n